"Dennis Rogers is as refreshing as a chew of tobacco."
— Jim Graham,
Commissioner of Agriculture

"Dennis Rogers is a homespun, down-to-earth fellow who knows what life is all about in North Carolina."
— Slim Short,
WNCT-TV, Greenville

"The News and Observer without Dennis Rogers is like a chitlin strut without collards and cornbread. What with increasing prices in women, whiskey and gasoline, Dennis is a bargain, triple distilled."
— Roy Wilder Jr., author,
"Y'all Spoken Here"

"Every day, Dennis Rogers reminds us all that the real world is made up of people who don't usually get their names in the newspapers. And after talking with people back home in Wilson County who knew Dennis when he was growing up, I can now say, without question, that he is the greatest living N&O columnist that Wilson County has ever produced."
— Jim Hunt,
Governor

"Dennis Rogers can be inspirational — when he wrote about his daughter growing up, I almost cried. But sometimes his writing is better. Basically, he's as comfortable and as welcome as a cold beer ... "
— Famous Bob Inskeep,
WRAL 101-FM, Raleigh

Home Grown

Dennis Rogers

The News and Observer

Raleigh, N.C.

This book is dedicated to Lelia Williamson Smith Lamm,
my Mama. She taught me, by her example, how to love.

Cole C. Campbell, editor.
David Martin, project coordinator.

Special thanks to the staff members of The News and Observer
Publishing Co. who assisted us in the creation of this book.

Cover photograph by Jackson Hill.

Contents

But First,
This Brief Message ...

Did you ever wonder what it would be like to have a dream come true, really happen just the way you hoped it would on those long nights when you are alone with your fantasies?

Well, let me tell you, it is wonderful.

The book you are holding is my fantasy come true. All writers dream that their work will have permanence. No matter how well journalists do their jobs, no matter how much of their sweat and soul goes into a story, they know in their hearts there is nothing more useless than yesterday's newspaper. It is a short trip from the front page to the bird cage.

But a book? Now that's a different matter. A book is permanent, it will be here for awhile. It may end up on the bottom shelf, way back in the cobwebs, but one day I'll walk into a library and there, thanks to the Dewey Decimal System, will be printed proof that once I wrote.

And if you don't think that's a kick, think again.

What's this book about? During the past three years I have written about 750 columns for The News and Observer, but this is not merely a collection of those pieces.

Rather, using material from those columns, we have tried to put together a tapestry, a portrait in many colors and textures, of what it was like to live in North Carolina in the latter part of the Seventies. By necessity, it is my view of our world, but I have tried to see our homeland with an eye toward the common experience, the things we have shared, the people we have known, the things we find preposterous, the things that anger us.

It is chock full of people, those remarkable people who have made this job possibly the best any journalist ever had, certainly the most incredible experience in my life.

There are lots of funny stories, the ones I lived and the ones I heard, the ones readers have said were their favorites.

But be warned, there are sad stories, stories that might anger you, stories you might not want to read again, but take a look at them. Frankly, I hated collards the first time, too.

Let me take a moment of your time and talk about this column writing business. After spending eight years as a career military man, I decided early in 1970 that if I was ever to realize my dream of writing it was high time I got about it.

I chose journalism, a decision I have never regretted. I have rightly been accused of being a somewhat naive idealist, but to me there is no higher calling than the truth and that's what journalism comes down to. We don't always do it as well as we should, and what we tell you might not always be what you want to know, but I have never known a journalist who would knowingly tell a lie to his readers.

Mine is a specialized form of journalism. I try to inform, but more importantly, I try to entertain. If you happen to learn something in the process, both of us are better for it.

I have driven close to 100,000 miles in the past three years, or roughly four times around the world, all of it in North Carolina. I have stayed in more motel rooms than I can count, eaten more restaurant meals than I care to remember and spent a sizable chunk of The News and Observer's money in the process.

There have been good days, many of them, and there have been days when I was so wiped out all I could do was stare at a blank piece of paper. The columns reflected those changes of mood. There is nowhere to hide when you write a daily column. It has all hung out in the open, the good columns and the turkeys, and bless you all, you've hung in there through the gobblers.

Putting together this book has been the high point of my career. And I want you to stick with me one more time so I can say thanks to some people who have put up with a lot and still remain my friends.

Cole Campbell kept this project going when even I was ready to give up. He is the creative genius behind it. He is a gentle giant. I'm glad he was there.

News and Observer Publisher Frank Daniels Jr. went against the advice of almost everyone and said "Yes" when I most needed to hear it.

Dave Martin and his calculator kept up with the bills. He has nickled and dimed me to death and has handed me a book I am proud of.

Dale Gibson is my best friend and my editor. His good sense, friendship and loyalty have seen me through some stormy times. For three years he has taken the raw material I gave him and made me look good. He is a professional, I know no higher compliment.

Robert Brooks, my managing editor, called me into his office three years ago and told me I was to start writing a daily column. He never asked me if I wanted the job and for that I am grateful, for if given a chance I would have run back to the safety of the newsroom. He takes a lot of chances every day putting out a newspaper I am proud to say I work for. He took a big chance, and then he gave me freedom, for both of those I am grateful.

The staff of The News and Observer, editors and reporters, are the finest journalists I know. Eastern North Carolina is well served by their combined efforts. I hope they know how good they are. I have stolen more good ideas from them than I will ever admit.

There have been many others who helped. Gene Hair believed in me, Jim Shumaker gave me my first job and yelled at me until I got it right, Sharon Shaw read the early stuff and didn't make fun of it although she had every reason to, the faculty and staff of the School of Journalism at the University of North Carolina came through with money, encouragement and guidance when I needed it most.

And my friends, the softball players, the Saturday night

party bunch, the winners and sinners, they listened to me brag and bitch and I've done far too much of both.

My family, Claudia, Denise and Melanie, have stood by me a long time. Without them, none of it would have had meaning or worth.

But it is the readers I thank most of all, the regulars who read my column day in and day out, the hundreds of people who have taken the time to tell me their story, the thousands who have written or called with encouragement and criticism, it is to all of you that I owe my allegiance and gratitude.

Now read the book.

Right Off the Top

For lack of a more precise definition, we will call it The Liver Lie.

Simply put, The Liver Lie says that anything that is really bad to you must be good for you.

Like liver.

When I was young, my sneaky grandmother used to say, "Eat this, it's good for you,"while on my plate she slapped a really nasty looking piece of liver.

"But it tastes terrible,"I would protest.

"I know, but it's good for you,"she'd say.

Who would have ever thought that a lovable granny, complete with hugs, glasses and white hair, would lie to an innocent kid like that?

Liver is not good for you. It is terrible for you. It makes your hair fall out and your toenails grow crooked. It will take the plaque off your teeth, make rust grow on your car and it makes you tell lies.

And it tastes awful. Even people who eat it don't really like it. They always come up with the same sad excuses.

"Fix it right and it's delicious," they say. "Your problem is you've never had it fixed right."

"Try it with onions,"another will suggest.

"I like it with a lot of catsup on it," says another.

Well, if it is so yummy, why in the heck do you have to disguise the taste with onions or catsup or frying it till it smokes and curls? Rib eye steaks are good barely cooked, so why isn't liver?

"But it's good for you," they will say in exasperation after you have deflated their myths. That's what they've been told. Not one out of a thousand has checked to see. They bought the big lie all the way.

There are other things that fit into The Liver Lie.

There are those in our midst who swear that jogging is good for you and I must admit that for a while I, too, was captivated by their siren song of pounding feet.

I bought myself some striped jogging shoes with a hip name, got me some old tattered running shorts and laid out a route that wound through attractive neighborhoods.

For months I followed the routine and each night I came back home, smelling like three weeks in a locker room, my knees and ankles throbbing, my chest feeling like it had been used for practice by the 82nd Airborne Division and saying to myself, boy, this must be good for me.

Jogging will not make you live forever.

It just seems like forever.

Look at a neighborhood jogger. He looks like he should be buried, gasping for air, stumbling along, dodging cars, dogs, gutter grates, low limbs and claiming it's fun.

It isn't. It is much more fun to come home, open the libation of your choosing and plop down on the sofa and watch the news.

The Liver Lie is everywhere. I avidly read book reviews and invariably, if I buy the books that come highly recommended, they turn out to be crashing bores. But I read them, thinking that somehow I should. They must be good for me. They aren't. All too often "great" books are tedium unending.

All Robert Altman movies, with the exception of "M.A.S.H.," are the cinematic versions of The Liver Lie. Anything that dull must have deep meaning. But it really doesn't. You thought it was dull because it was.

Discos are The Liver Lie set to music. Somehow it has

been decided that buying a lot of artificial clothes, blow-drying your hair until it smolders, paying a hefty admission price, entering a room full of smoke and mediocre music so loud it will melt steel and then jumping up and down for several hours somehow makes you a better person.

It does not. It makes you sweaty, hung over, broke and deaf. Enjoy it if you care to, but don't tell me it is enlightening.

The Liver Lie is everywhere. It includes running up the stairs in your office building (silly when there is a perfectly good elevator), listening to boring politicians, sending out Christmas cards, making long-distance calls after midnight when the rates are cheaper (which is more important, three minutes to Moscow for $2 or sleep?) and extra-firm mattresses.

No more. If it is not fun, if it does not taste good, if it does not make you feel better instantly, then to heck with it.

Good Buddy & Co.

As a concerned citizen, I figured it was my duty to drop by the governor's office the other day to look around and watch our tax dollars at work.

Our tax dollars were in a tizzy.

Stephanie Bass, the governor's deputy press secretary, is an old buddy of mine; we went hungry together while in Journalism School in Chapel Hill. Stephanie, in a futile effort to keep the wolves from the door, worked in the school office. I hung around waiting for someone to leave change in the cracker machine.

I am happy to report that Stephanie is doing better now. She didn't offer to buy me lunch or give me an all-expenses-paid junket to Pactolus, which is what I'm told goes on in the rarified air of big-time guvmint, but she did point to the coffee machine when I walked in.

"Any particular cup?" I asked, reaching automatically for a lovely Carolina blue mug.

"No," she said, looking just a tad worried, "But the one you're holding belongs to the governor."

I dropped that cup like it was dipped in PCBs. I fully expected an enraged SBI agent the size of a small car to leap from a desk drawer and gun me down if I so much as sipped a slurp from Good Buddy's cup.

I must explain. I am not being disrespectful when I call Gov. James B. Hunt Jr. Good Buddy. Heck, anybody from Wilson County is fine by me, but those who know him well are aware that he used to have a habit of calling everyone "Good Buddy" while he was campaigning.

I am not one who knows the governor well, though I keep trying to convince him we're kin, but he won't admit it. You never know when something like that will come in handy, although the last time I mentioned it to him my car flunked its annual inspection the next day. I'm not making any accusations, you understand, but you never know.

Anyway, to the press, being nasty folks, Hunt has been nicknamed "Good Buddy." I hear he hates it, so sorry Cousin Gov.

"We've figured out what to do with PCBs," press secretary Gary Pearce announced. "How's that for a scoop?"

I knew it was a setup. The day has not come when a press secretary will give a scoop to a columnist who is in charge of massive silliness.

"We've figured out that one PCB won't hurt you, so we're asking for volunteers statewide to eat one PCB each," Pearce said. "The governor is going to eat the first one himself, on TV. Would you like to volunteer?"

I declined. If he won't claim kin, to heck with him.

Gary and I agreed that we have a problem with PCBs. That nasty stuff is no laughing matter, but we can't help personalizing the things. I get this mental image of tiny little fellows with tiny little hats and tiny little trench coats on a rampage along our roadsides.

"Look, there's a PCB now," I can hear a trooper say just before he jumps out and beats the critter to a tiny little pulp with his billy club.

A month ago I'd never heard of a PCB. Now I'm scared to death of them. Ain't progress wonderful?

"You think we've got it bad," Pearce said. "Up in Michigan, they've got to worry about PBBs."

"Lord, what are they?" I asked.

"Beats me, but they come first in the alphabet, so they

must be terrible, worse than PCBs.''

Meanwhile, Stephanie was beating a tape cassette to death on her desk.

"Thing's stuck," she said with a growl. "Sometimes this helps. I've got to feed the radio stations, and I'm going CRAZY."

Stephanie speaks in capital letters when her voice rises to painful levels. I didn't ask her what she was going to feed the microphone boys. I was afraid of the answer.

"What I want to know, Pearce, is why my column is not included in the daily news summary that goes to the governor?" I demanded. "I write about important stuff."

The summary, by the way, is copies of all important news stories from all over the state, clipped for the governor so he can spend more time with the comics.

"No need to," Pearce said. "The governor reads your column first thing every day."

"Glib, Pearce, really glib."

"Yeah, and did you know that glib spelled backwards is very close to bilge?" Pearce asked.

We all know what is at the end of the oft-mentioned campaign trail — fame, power and glory.

But what is at the beginning of the campaign trail? Indeed, where is the campaign trail? I'd read about it but I hadn't seen it. It isn't on any map, the fellows at AAA weren't any help at all and the good buddies on my CB fell flat.

But, as you probably have figured out by now, I have finally found it, being the frustrated political reporter that I am and being envious of those who get to use political cliches all the time.

The campaign trail begins in the rain forest of Jones County. There is where you will find the supersecret CIA.

The CIA — Cliche Indoctrination Academy — is a school for would-be power wielders. Every candidate I've run across is a graduate, but don't expect them to admit it.

But there are ways to tell. Does your candidate claim to

be the candidate of the people? Does he or she claim to know not only what the grass roots are but to actually be in touch with them? Does his or her lips pucker anytime they get within three feet of an unslobbered-upon baby? Do they want the job?

If so, you can bet your ballot they are CIA plants.

Using infiltration techniques taught me by a mystic aluminum siding salesman, I recently sneaked into the CIA. Here is my report:

The first place I went was the wardrobe department, where male candidates are outfitted in those lovely matching blue suits we have all come to loathe. Once fitted, they practice throwing their jackets over their shoulders and rolling up their sleeves while saying, "I understand your problems" to every occupational, social, racial, religious or ethnic group in sight. To get a passing grade they must keep a straight face while doing all this.

From there I went to the industrial arts department, where the candidates were busy hammering out positions. As soon as they were all hammered out, the candidates went outdoors and staked out their positions.

Another group was working real hard, putting together platforms, plank by plank.

I don't know what it means either, but that's the way they talk.

Athletics play a big part at the CIA. One of the more popular classes consisted of candidates walking across a cow pasture, trying to keep from stepping in what they would later try to sell us, while all the time they had their coats slung over their shoulders, their sleeves rolled up and maintained a distant, dedicated look in their eyes. It is not an easy task.

On one side of the athletic field were men and women straddling fences, another popular class, and in the nearby woods, other candidates ran hard, trying to avoid thorny issues and not trip over the grass roots. Once a candidate tired, he took to the stump.

But the most popular activity of all, the one that everyone promised to stay away from but to which all were eventually drawn, was mud slinging.

Don't you love those words "mud slinging"? Doesn't it

sound like fun?

There they stood one on one, eyeball to eyeball, toe to toe, candidates possessed, as the mud flew. The activity was made even more difficult when each candidate was made to repeat, "I will not resort to mud slinging during this campaign" as he or she slung away.

There were other activities too numerous to mention, such as playing on a campaign swing, the throwing of hats into rings, waffling and flip flopping, the picking of nits, the splitting of hairs and the ever popular "going down to the wire."

Remember, vote early and often.

Roll Over, Bogey

It was going to be a tough case, I knew that. It was in her eyes.

She was in trouble. But then, I'm used to ladies in trouble.

"There is no one else to turn to," the lady said, looking at me like a just-whipped dog. "I can't go to the police. I've heard you'll take the tough cases, the kind no one else will touch. They say you're the best private eye in town."

She was good, I had to hand her that. She knew I was a sucker for dames in a jam. My lip curled behind the cigarette smoke.

"Give it to me straight," I said, kicking the desk drawer that held the gin and the gat. "No lies, doll. I've had enough lying women to last me a long time."

"I want you to find spring," she said, the words gushing out. "Spring is missing. She is due to arrive this week, but no one has seen her. Usually she comes by a little in advance, you know, just to tell us she's okay, but this year? Nothing."

"Okay, Toots, I'll take the case," I snarled, hoping this was almost over because my lip was getting tired of curling. "Now who gets the bill?"

"Send it to me," she said, "Send it to Mother Nature."

"Okay, Mom, you're on. Now get outa here, I got work to do," I said, kicking over the coat rack and punching my tough fist through the wall, just for practice.

I left my grimy office and headed off to find her. I didn't tell Mom Nature, but this one looked hopeless. But I'm used to hopeless cases. They're my specialty.

"She was here but she's gone," a guy told me in Bunn. "She said for us to get this here baseball field ready to play so I guess she means to come back."

I almost had her between Crisp and Fountain. I saw a Granny in a sunbonnet, stooped low over a flower bed.

"Yep, she was here this morning," the old woman said. "We had us a real nice visit but she had to leave. As soon as she left I came out here and started piddling in my flowers. But she said she'd be back."

Coming through Lizzie I thought I had her for sure. I stopped at a crossroads store, but there was just a kid.

"It was the dangdest thing," he said. "All the boys were sitting around like they always do when spring blew by here in a flat-out hurry. Just had time to wave.

"And every one of them old boys got in their pickups and headed home. In an hour they were in the fields, plowing like crazy."

I spent a restless night in Kinston. This case was getting to me, but then they always do. I may look tough, but I have a soft heart for ladies in a fix.

"She's waiting for you at Cliffs of the Neuse State Park," a pretty girl whispered while I drank java and read the paper. "She said to hurry. She said you'd know what to do."

I hurried. On the way, I found her trail. Clouds the size of mountains played dodgeball with the sun. Dust from just-plowed fields blew across the road. It was going to be close.

The people in the park had seen her. Two guys played with a Frisbee. Two girls and a guy watched the river boil past, yellow and angry.

I walked up a trail. Something told me where she'd be.

"Psst, over here," said a voice like a song.

I followed the sound and there she was, sitting on a seat of Spanish moss and smiling up at me.

"You the guy looking for me?" she asked.

"Yeah lady, I'm the guy," I answered. I tried to snarl

but my heart wasn't in it.

"You go back and tell 'em I'm all right," she said, and the trees sang. "I know it's been rough, but tell them to be patient. This is going to be the best ever, and it'll be worth the wait. You tell them that for me."

And she was gone. A breeze came by and took her away leaving nothing but the smell of her perfume and a soft kiss on my cheek.

I smiled. Another tough case broken.

Just a Friendly Game

I have come to realize, as I think about it in the few moments when the pain clears and my mind will allow me to think of something besides learning how to walk, that an evil force lurks in the spring air.

Each spring, as the daffodils stand tall and pollen covers the earth, this evil force seeps quietly into the brain and drives normally sane people to do things they wouldn't normally consider.

I speak, of course, of softball.

You remember softball. It happened to all of us. It was physical education class and the announcement was made that today, we will play softball.

Why softball and not baseball, the all-American sport?

Then they gave us the big lie.

Play softball, they said, because the ball is soft and it won't hurt you. You can catch a softball with your bare hands. If it hits you in the face it will not take a second mortgage on your house to repair the damage.

Tell that to Cole Campbell and Howard Goldberg.

Cole and Howard were the only obvious victims of the first seasonal softball game between reporters and copy editors at The News and Observer.

I write this as a public service. All over the state, one group is busy challenging another group to a friendly softball game. Maybe our experience will help you come to your senses.

We were driven from our homes to meet at high noon on a dusty softball field to settle once and for all the softball championship of the universe, press division.

On the good guys team, made up of writers, were such sports incompetents as Bruce "The Guce" Siceloff; Dale "Hoot" Gibson, state editor and (he thinks) team captain; Richard Whittle, Howard, Cole, yours truly and a bunch of ridiculously young and robust (but equally incompetent) copy boys.

On the copy editor's team were such hotshots as Big John Bartosek, the only man alive who can play softball while wearing a wide-brimmed cowboy hat; Lynn Medford, who looks like Little Orphan Annie and throws a mean pitch; Garnet Bass, a premier brunswick stew cook; Betsy Robertson, a vicious baserunner whom I may never forgive for stepping on my foot as she beat out a grounder to first; Mac McGrew, a gray-haired demon at shortstop, and a host of even more of the copy boys.

It was not a pretty game. But it was memorable.

Who can forget the sterling moment when Campbell defied physics (and good sense) and kissed a sizzling foul tip. He walked off the field with a permanent pucker in his upper lip. The doctor says the swelling will go down. Don't count on it.

Then there was Goldberg. His trick was to stop a toss to second by catching it with the end of his thumb. Now there is a permanent dimple in our only softball and Goldberg swears his thumb used to be longer than it is now, but you know how Duke University people are.

Personally, I thought he looked nifty with a thumb the size and color of a fat grape.

It goes without saying that the good guys won, which is the way things should be.

After a couple of hours — we never could figure out what inning it was — we quit the game with the good guys leading 20 to 10.

The copy editors, as might be expected, said we forfeited the game when our team showed up an hour late, so I guess we'll have to do it all again.

But that is in the future. Now I'm busy searching for a miracle cure for aching eyebrows and sprained hair.

In fact, the only thing that doesn't hurt is my right foot,

the one Betsy crushed.

But when the feeling comes back, it probably will too.

Skin and Bones

I am a member of an oppressed minority.

Many of you are, as well, but you've never realized it.

How can you tell?

Has anyone ever walked up to you and said, "How in the world do you stay so thin?"

Or maybe they hit you with the ever-popular, "Have you always been so thin?"

If so, then you are skinny, my friend. Not thin nor trim nor svelte nor even lean. I'm talking about skinny.

Skinny people are treated as embarrassments to their families. Mothers take it as a personal affront, feeling they must have failed somewhere "to fatten that kid up."

If you are tired of it, as I am, then you are ready to join with your fellow skinnies and stop all this harassment merely because we are lucky enough to weigh less than a 1954 DeSoto.

Rise up, Ribs. Be brave, Bones. Cast off those shackles. Don't ever feel guilty about dessert again.

Join THIN.

What is THIN, you ask? It stands for "Thank Heaven I'm Normal" and, since I am the skinniest person I know of, I am the founder and, so far, the only member.

Our goal is to put an end to the conspiracy that is afoot in our fair land. We all know who is behind it. It is the work of The Chubbies.

They are trying their rotund best to make it hard on us light-footed folks.

When is the last time you tried to find a size 35-long coat in a men's store? There are plenty of sizes big enough to double as a tent for three Cub Scouts but for us normal-sized folks the only thing in stock is either black or double-breasted.

It gets embarrassing to shop in the boys' department, as we are often forced to do. The scent of bubble gum in the dressing room is overpowering.

Everything you see in the grocery stores these days proudly proclaims itself "low calorie.'

I do not want beer with half as many calories. I want beer with twice as many.

Have you ever eaten a low-calorie (Gag ... there's that word again) dessert? It tastes like flat water.

Take a Chubbie to a restaurant and ask him about dessert and he will invariably say, "No thanks, I'm watching my weight, but you go right ahead."

So there you sit, strawbery shortcake and a double handful of whipped cream in front of you and your appetite ruined by guilt.

Who, I ask you, are the nation's sex symbols?

Do girls write mash notes to Don Knotts of Barney Fife fame? Did you ever see a sexy poster of Woody Allen? Of course not. Even Cher is in eclipse.

If I see one more book on how to lose weight I'm going to kick a well-upholstered Chubbie.

But there is something you can do. Join THIN.

No more will we take their insults. When asked, "Don't you eat?," answer, "Of course not. Food has not passed my lips in eight years."

Walk up to a Chubbie and say, "Have you always been fat? What's the matter? Do you eat all the time?"

Then they'll know how it feels.

Eat fattening foods and relish them. Ask for seconds when The Chubbies are eating salads. When you walk into a store and can't find clothes that fit, say, "I'm sorry, I didn't know you catered only to fat people."

Wear your bathing suit proudly. Show those knobby knees, spindly legs and rippling ribs and threaten to stab them with a pointy elbow if they laugh.

Now I'm going to lunch and eat bread and potatoes and have sugar in my iced tea and then a double helping of dessert and I plan to do absolutely no exercise.

This is war, remember, and we must be strong.

To the Barricades

One by one, with hardly a whimper to disturb our pell-mell rush to the brighter day that is deservedly our fate, our freedoms are dying.

They started falling by the wayside when people began moving within killing distance of each other, for when man must concern himself with anything other than his own self-styled survival, he gives up a bite-sized chunk of his freedom.

But since it is more convenient to live together than apart, we choose to give up freedoms for the sake of harmony.

I promised not to dump PCBs on my neighbor's lawn and he promised not to fire a machine gun into my bedroom, that sort of thing. So far, so good.

But then it got one-sided. We started giving up more than we were getting.

For instance, beats there a heart so ecologically pure that the stingy-sweet smell of burning leaves is not soothing?

A crisp, deep blue day, a warm sweater, a smooth rake handle, fluffy leaves — surely a recipe for peace of mind.

But to have to jam all those lovely leaves into a sickly green plastic bag that reeks of a chemistry lab is unquestionably a sin.

Not to be allowed to burn leaves is to be driven from the theater before the final curtain, to have the lights go out in the seventh inning, to lose a sneeze somewhere between "ah" and "choo."

But we let them do it to us. Now they are at it again. This time they must be stopped, freedom-lovers. To the barricades.

Our city parents — you can't use that time-worn "city fathers" anymore, what with a woman mayor and a woman council member, and "city persons" doesn't seem to get it either — are in a royal dither these days over dog droppings.

Now this is serious stuff, so please don't laugh. It seems that suddenly people are concerned about other folks' dogs coming into their yards and leaving them little surprise presents in unexpected places, like on the route to the mail box or in the driveway.

It is a pooper-scooper law, if you will, which means that if your mutt answers nature's call on your neighbor's lawn, you will have to boogie over with your little shovel and remove the offending evidence.

Exactly how violators will be identified is not clear yet. Does that pile belong to Spot or Fifi? You can see the problem. After all, we aren't dealing with fingerprints or license numbers here. You've seen one, you've seen 'em all, but I'm sure this can be worked out.

This being a democracy and all, I decided that someone should ask the dogs what they think of this turn of events. After all, they are the ones who will be affected.

So I asked Maggie the Marvelous Mutt what she thought about it.

It took her an impolite time to stop laughing. She'd missed the papers and hadn't heard about the proposed law.

"Let me see if I have this straight," she said, daintily wiping the last of her Kennel-Ration from her mouth. She is such a lady. "They're saying that when I have to do something disgusting, I have to do it at home?"

Yep, I told her, that's about it.

"Why, I think it is wonderful," Maggie said.

I told her I was surprised she would favor the law, since she is of a wandering nature at times and it could be a long trot home.

"That just shows how much you know about the law," Maggie said. Maggie is pretty smart. "Sure, it will be inconvenient, but look at the legal precedent it would set. If they start controlling all the disgusting things in the world — and I'll be the first one to admit that stepping in a little pile is pretty gross — think of all the things they could get rid of.

"For instance, you know those foul-talking women in stores on Saturdays who jerk their kids around like they were cannon lanyards? Gone in a heartbeat.

"And how about all those ugly women who wear hair curlers in public? Lying here chewing on my bones, I have often wondered where in the world they were going at night that could be so important they would go out in public in the daytime and let people see them like that."

"Now Maggie," I cautioned, "Women aren't the only ones who do disgusting things in public. Men can get pretty crude, too. Let's not get sexist here."

"Cool it, skinny, I'm getting to you guys," she said. "Have you taken a look at yourself in a bathing suit anytime lately? And what about those guys who let their pants hang down under their fat bellies and scratch a lot? Yuck City!

And what about those jerks who ride down the road in jacked-up cars, scaring the bejeezus out of me with their loud mufflers and throwing beer cans out the window? Certainly if they can identify dog droppings they can find fingerprints on those beer cans, can't they?"

I sensed Maggie was losing control. I tried to leave the yard, but she bared her teeth.

"It is a wonderful law," she said. "If we can rid the world of dog droppings, can campaign posters be far behind?

"And what about birds? Those twittering fools live in nests, you know, and nests are in trees and trees are on someone's property. If a bird who lives in a neighbor's yard flies over and decorates your car windshield, won't it be great to invite the neighbor over to have him wash the car for free?

"Just think of all the sickening things we could remove from Raleigh. Like cats who stand outside my fence and drive me crazy and people who pick their noses while sitting at stoplights when they think no one sees them or people who burp where they shouldn't."

"But Maggie, you don't understand, they aren't talking about all the disgusting things in the world," I told her, "just one disgusting thing. Dog do-do, Maggie, that's the issue here."

"Don't count on it, knobby knees," she said. "Today dog do-do, tomorrow perfection."

About then I sneezed, a big honker.

"You're next," Maggie grinned.

War, Pain and V-I-C-T-O-R-Y

Everyone I know has seen "Star Wars," the biggest money-making movie of all time, and already people are looking forward to the sequel, due out anytime.

I loved the movie so I decided to use all my reporter tricks and find out what the sequel will be about.

It's about two hours long.

Having obtained the only copy of the script in existence, I can now reveal the plot, such as it is:

The music swells, the house lights dim and the movie begins ...

A long time ago in a galaxy far, far away ... STAR WARTS.

Princess Lulu Belle Johnson, a night-shift waitress at a pancake house on U.S. 301, has escaped from the ominous Imperial Meanies. She has uncovered a really nasty plot to infect downtown Smithfield with ugly warts by hiding all known bottles of Wart Off and replacing them with Frog Juice.

Needless to say, the Imperial Meanies try to stop her and she turns to her trusty robots, Fred and Ethel, for help. These are not your garden variety robots, however. Fred is a garage door opener and Ethel is a rental carpet shampooer.

The robots escape with the plan in the back of a Greyhound bus and find their way east where a young hog farmer from Camden County named Marvin Cornstalker finds them. Having neither a garage nor a carpet, Cornstalker tries to throw them out as junk, only to be interrupted by Boop Boop Be Doop Kentucky, a retired dermatologist.

Boop figures out what is going on and teaches Marvin the secrets of The Farce, a mystical power that teaches you how to laugh uproariously in the face of danger.

They get in Marvin's 1954 blue pickup truck, with Fred and Ethel in the back, and go off to fight the Imperial Meanies, protect Smithfield from Star Warts, rescue Princess LuLu, and fight the dreaded Dearth Valor, commander of the hated "Heavy Chevy" from Fayetteville.

Dearth and the Heavy Chevy, a candy-apple red monster with dual exhausts, tires three feet wide and the back jacked up so high you have to wear seat belts to keep from sliding into the foot, are busy at work spreading warts all over Johnston County in preparation for their heinous attack on downtown Smithfield.

Things don't go well for Marvin and Boop. It rains and Fred and Ethel rust where they sit, Princess Lulu decides Marvin is a flaming nerd and won't have anything to do with him, Boop spends most of the movie rubbing Ben Gay on his aching joints and smoking Camels and it is certainly looking bad.

Marvin's pickup is right on the verge of being melted by the exhaust gases from the Heavy Chevy when, Lo and behold, out of the tobacco fields roars Bolt Upright, the hero, who has been disguised as a mild-mannered columnist for a Raleigh newspaper.

Bolt wins Princess Lulu's favors, she tells him the secret of the Heavy Chevy, he puts Boop in a Home for the Terminally Bewildered, throws Fred and Ethel in the trash where they have belonged all along and then pours sugar in the gas tank of the Heavy Chevy while Dearth Valor is in the Dew Drop Inn having a bag of Beer Nuts.

Johnston County residents, thankful at having been saved, bestow great honors on Bolt, Lulu and Marvin, rescue Fred and Ethel and make can openers of them, ignore Boop completely and make the world's weirdest planter out of the Heavy Chevy.

I hope I didn't spoil it for you. It will be opening soon at a theater near you. Don't miss it.

It occurred to me, lying here in my backless hospital gown with my mind whacked out on pain killer, that for every brilliant doctor who graduates at the top of his class from the nation's best medical school, there is a yo-yo who graduates from the bottom of his class at the nation's worst medical school.

Think about that the next time your doctor gives you a prescription.

I did a lot of thinking about doctors and hospitals. I had

to spend three days in the hospital when my lung went "pssst" and collapsed on me. There is very little else to think about at such times, other than trying to remember how to breathe.

I have, for instance, finally figured out why nurses wake you up every two hours during the night. They pretend they want to take your blood pressure and stuff like that, but their real reason is very simple.

They want to know if you're still alive.

Hospital beds are at a premium these days, and think of the waste to have a dead body taking up a $100-a-day room. At that price, you want to make sure the guy still is able to pay his bill.

And I have learned how to understand what hospital people mean when they talk. Not what they say, what they really mean.

"Now you might feel this a little," the doctor says, when what he really means is, "Sharpen your fingernails, hoss, 'cause this is gonna make you hang from the ceiling."

"Now, that wasn't too bad, was it?" the doctor says once his probing, gouging, cutting, pulling and temporary maiming has stopped. "Have I killed you?" is what he's really saying, so answer him quickly and make at least one of you feel better.

"Hate to bother you so early, but we need to take your temperature," the cheery nurse bellows at 6 a.m., when what she means is, "Look sucker, if I've got to be up at this ungodly hour, so do you."

"This won't take but a minute," the business office lady tells you at check-out time. Of course it won't take long. Armed robbery never does.

"You wanna TV? We only rent them one day at a time, cash in advance," the woman says, meaning, "Look buster, you don't look like you're going to make it until tomorrow, so pay up now."

And the ever-popular 'How are you this morning?" really means "You ain't dead yet?"

What this world needs is more cheerleaders.

We have enough sourpusses standing around saying it won't work.

No matter what happens, from peace prospects in the Middle East to the latest gizmo to clean your grungy oven, there is always a bunch of naysayers standing around to shake their ugly heads and pout just because they didn't think of it first.

So I am proposing that we have more cheerleaders.

I don't mean cheerleaders in general, I mean cheerleaders specifically. I'm talking Dallas Cowgirls, I'm talking Chargettes of San Diego. I mean luscious, non-liberated hunks with skimpy little costumes. I'm talking cheerleaders, boys and girls. I want to see some pom poms.

Being the honest, hard-working fellow I am, I freely admit to having borrowed this concept from a colleague, Bob Greene of Chicago. But all Greene suggested is that journalists have cheerleaders like those NFL ladies, which I think is a terrible idea. Why should the press be the only ones to enjoy having cheerleaders pulling for them when all the rest of the world is slaving away in cheerless gloom?

No, I am a democrat (small d, you notice) and I want to spread the wealth. I think everybody ought to have a cheerleader.

For instance, we are announcing formation of Hunt's Honeys. The Honeys will gather each morning at Gov. James B. Hunt Jr.'s front door and cheer him off to work. When His Excellency trots off on his morning jog, the Honey's will form a double line on either side of the street and yell things like, "Go Guv, Go Guv." You get the idea.

And when His Excellency gets to the office, the Honeys will be there to yell, "Make That Speech, Sign That Letter. We All Know, Hunt is Better ... Yeah Jim."

Now doesn't that have a nice ring to it?

Bankers could have girls in pinstriped vests and wing tip shoes, to be called Changettes, in the lobby yelling, "Close That Deal, Make A Dollar, All For Money, Stand Up and Holler."

And don't forget plumbers. Here I propose that all short girls, the kind who have been grumbling about not being tall and slinky enough to wear Annie Hall clothes, be outfitted in tiny little coveralls. They will be known as the Wrenches. They will then gather under the house with the plumbers and cheer them on with things like, "Tighten That Pipe, Melt That Lead, But Be Careful, Don't Bump Your Head."

And who among us needs cheerleaders more than farmers?

Here we will have a group of girls who look like Lt. Gov. James C. Green, who also happens to own a few tobacco warehouses. (Only girls who smoke 17 packs of cigarettes a day need apply.) The Greenettes will stand at the end of the row and as the tractor nears, will croak, "Plow It Again, Plow It Again, Straighter, Straighter" or, just to keep some variety here, "Plant That Corn, Sow That Bean, Sell Your Tobacco With Jimmy Green."

And teachers, bless their chalk dust hearts, need more help than even I could give. Here I propose that we have cheerleaders dressed in sexy costumes on which are printed all the answers to the new state competency test.

The Eraserettes will cheer our teachers on to greater heights of intellectual achievement by yelling, "Practice Those Verbs Or We'll All Be Sunk, Come On, Teach, Don't Let Them Flunk."

All girls wishing to become cheerleaders are asked to contact this column with suggested cheers, costumes and area of specialty.

Auditions, with demonstrations by my own cheerleaders, known as Dennis' Dolls, will be held anon.

But to show you how devoted The Dolls are, here is their newest cheer, "Write That Column, You Skinny Slob, And Write It Well, Or You'll Lose Your Job."

Go team.

Good Days and Bad

Some things for which we should be thankful on this Thanksgiving Day: a baby's smile, a beautiful sunset, the love of friends and peace in the world.

Sure, I'm thankful for that stuff, as I'm sure you are, but there are a lot more things I wish I was thankful for.

For instance, I would be extremely grateful if Linda

Ronstadt worked at the next desk. It's not that I don't enjoy sitting next to Entertainment Editor Bill Morrison. But if Linda was there, why I'd go for her coffee, she would hum "Baby, Baby" all day and she'd loan me paper clips. I think that would be a wonderful way to pass my days.

I would give the best thank-you speech in the world if I won an Oscar for my sensitive performance in "The Don Knotts Story."

I would give a silent and heartfelt prayer of thanksgiving if someone would tell me how to carve a turkey without looking like I just went 15 rounds with a New York street gang and without reducing a $20 turkey to instant hash while my family cheerfully watches me make a fool of myself.

In fact, if they'd just grow a turkey that would patiently sit on the platter while I hacked away with my electric knife I would be mildly appreciative.

I would positively gush with joy if once, just once, my car would break down within pushing distance of a garage. My last broken-down episode resulted in a $20 towing charge so the mechanic could do $10 worth of work to replace a $3 wire. That, of course, followed by one day the $82 alternator caper.

I would leap for joy if a politician, of whatever stripe, would simply stand up and say, "I don't know," when asked what he would do to cure the nation's ills rather than having the public figure it out by trial and error.

Wouldn't it be lovely if liver tasted like anything else but liver?

I would offer a polite thank you every morning if some wizard engineer would invent a toothbrush that did not dribble white foam down my hand and forearm every time I brushed my teeth.

Gratitude would ooze from every pore if Willie Nelson would invite me to go on a weekend fishing trip with him and when it was over we'd drop over to Waylon Jennings's house for a cold, long-necked Lone Star.

All the world would be a better place, and the masses would raise their voices in joyous phrase if the word "boogie" was stricken from our collective tongue.

I would smile with grateful relief if one night Walter

Cronkite would come on the tube and say "Well, nothing happened today, so we're going to show you a rerun of 'Dobie Gillis' instead."

It would be a day of rejoicing if, come tax time, the Internal Revenue Service would come by the house and say, "Sir, you've had a rough year so here's a bag of money."

But just so this doesn't sound like sour grapes, there are three things for which I am grateful this Thanksgiving.

First of all, I'm grateful that the Redskins and the Cowboys are playing on TV this afternoon.

Secondly, I am grateful for the pencil, one of the very few things in this technological age that never has a new, improved, better-than-ever model each year. It quietly does its job and when it is all gone, you throw it away. It is efficient and cheap. It does not leak, the spring does not break, the felt-tip point does not get all squishy and it never runs out.

Thirdly, and most importantly, I am grateful for the first person who ever ate an egg. Think about that. Some man or woman saw a chicken lay an egg, saw where it came from, and still said, "Hey, I think I'll eat that thing." And then, when he or she realized you had to peel it first, opened it up, saw that mess inside, and still ate it.

That is true bravery and deserving of our thanks.

Dear Friends:

Knowing how busy all of us are, once again we will share our family's year by way of our annual Christmas letter.

It has been a delightful year for all of us. Bubba got out of jail in the spring!

That mean old judge who sent dear Bubba up to the Big House for his tiny little mistake of driving his tractor through the Methodist Women's Sewing Circle and then doing a wheelie on Mrs. Ledbetter's foot was certainly unkind, wasn't he?

Bubba said it was all right with him, though, since he didn't remember the tractor incident at all, much less Mrs. Ledbetter's foot. But Bubba did say he seemed to recall throwing that run-over possum to the chairwoman as he lapped the room.

Bubba's girlfriend is doing real well on her job down to the Quickie Dog out on the bypass. Ethel Grace looks cute in her beehive hairdo and Smile button. It was some fun, I'll tell you, when she put three tablespoons of garlic instead of onions on Mayor Billy Bob's double cheeseburger that day when his pickup stopped off the campaign trail for lunch. Mayor Billy Bob said he had a heck of time getting folks to stand still long enough to listen to him for the next week or so.

We are having some trouble this year with Junior. I don't know what's gotten into the boy. I thought he had quit dipping Tube Rose snuff until that time the football coach slapped him on the back and Junior danged near passed away.

But old Junior charged into that game and kissed the other quarterback smack on the mouth. The quarterback — pretty much of a sissy, I think — left the game for good and our side won.

Then our team picked Junior up on their shoulders and took him off the field.

We haven't found him yet, but we're still looking.

Some good news. Uncle Rafer is working again. You can't hardly see that dent in his head from when the mule kicked him a year ago this coming March.

Bless his heart, he's trying, but he does get confused. Last week he went coon hunting. Now we've got three big coons in the dog pen, but it's no problem, since Old Blue is still at the vet. The vet says he hopes he can get all the buckshot out of him by spring.

Old Sally, I'm sorry to report, went straight to doggie heaven.

I don't know what's gotten into Aunt Louise, though. She used to be such a sweet woman. She says that if Uncle Rafer ever lets her out of the closet, where he put her on a hanger during one of his "forgetful times," she's going to have him put away.

Judy Lynn has had another young 'un. That makes eight, I think, and all of them have real good names. She named them all after family members. There's Billy Joe, Joe Bobby, Billy Bobby, Jim Johnny Paul, Paul Bobby Joe, Jimmy Bobby Paul, Paul Jimmy John and Johnny Jimmy Joe Paul Fred.

Everyone is certainly looking forward to Old Saint Nick. Oscar said he'd paint all the tires around the trees with a new coat of whitewash, so the place should have a real festive look.

Maybe it will be better than last year. You'll remember that Oscar got to having a few with the boys down to the filling station and came home and mixed gasoline with the whitewash before he painted the house.

The firemen said it was the biggest blaze they'd ever seen and if we hadn't saved Uncle Josh's teeth it would have been a total loss. Oh well, we can't let those little things get us down, can we?

But if I was you, I'd be careful where you flipped your butt come Christmas Day.

Little Betty Barbara is so excited! Bubba has promised her he'll take her braces off in time for Christmas morning. We all thought it was real sweet of Bubba to put the braces on her teeth before he was sent away for a year.

But Betty Barbara was a real hellion that day. Bubba got out the pliers, the baling wire and the soldering iron and I'll be danged if that Betty Barbara didn't take off like a shot. We had to chase her halfway to Old Man Buffkin's place before we could catch her and hold her down for Bubba.

But she looks real good, especially when she shines her braces with steel wool. We're just hoping she'll be able to talk again some day.

That's all from here. Hope you and yours have a fine time and if you see Junior, tell him to come home.

Merry Christmas!

I have this friend I hate.

He's a nice guy, plays golf as poorly as I do, enjoys the same kind of music and loves sports.

We spend a lot of time together, but the other day I had an urge to wrap a nine-iron around his ugly head.

"Got your Christmas shopping done yet?" I asked, fully expecting him to say, "Of course not," after which we'd fume about the commercialization of Christmas, how shopping was a pain in the wallet, or thereabouts, stuff that we sensitive people talk about this time of year.

"Yep, I'm finished, all done, bought it all," he said, gloating.

How dare he say something like that a full week before Christmas? Doesn't he know that the smart money never ventures forth until the last moment? What is he trying to do, ruin Christmas?

You see, shopping early for Christmas gifts is really dumb. The problem is, there is too much stuff to buy if you shop too early. And with all that stuff out there, there are no excuses for not buying exactly the right gift for everyone on your list.

When you've got a month, Hoss, it better be right.

But with us last-minute types, it is a different story. We are spared the agony of pawing through well-stocked shelves. People for whom we are shopping know we don't do it until the last minute and are thankful if they get anything at all, much less some exotic gadget that is just perfect.

For us it is simple: buy what the stores have.

Who cares if Auntie Alice doesn't want a wrench. Sorry, they were out of Ronco automatic egg scramblers.

Uncle Bob doesn't need a machine that will slice everything in the world, including making julienne fingers and decorative apple swirls? Too bad, the store was out of socks.

Actually, there is a lot of logic in doing it my way.

If you shop for days and find this perfectly divine sweater for Aunt Alice, a little number in puce and plum, and hand it to her at Christmas, she is going to go ga-ga over it, say it is just perfect and pack that bugger away before your car leaves the driveway.

But she won't tell you. She knows how hard you looked for it, and she'll be afraid of hurting your feelings.

But if you get her a wrench, she'll be down at the store

by dawn's early light exchanging it for something she wants.

So don't worry about shopping early. There is too much stuff, and it is confusing.

Buy them all a maroon, plastic bicycle seat.

And here's the best part, the bicycle seat department is never crowded.

I have ventured forth exactly once this holiday season. It was the day before yesterday. The evening began with high hopes and a moderate checkbook.

It ended with me saying unkind things to the Salvation Army bell ringer and snarling at Santa Claus.

I do not like crowds. I do not like people who push me around, especially grim-faced grannies with advanced degrees in elbow.

One clerk said, "Who's next?" and the answer, "I am," sounded like the Mormon Tabernacle Choir at full blast.

Standing at one end of a local shopping mall, I surveyed the scene before me. It looked like the set of a movie that could have been called, "Mayhem on the Mall."

"Jingle Bells" was playing in the bathroom, but the words that bounced around my shattered mind were different somehow.

So as the rush roars on, try my version, to the tune of "Jingle Bells":

"Jingle bells, jingle bells, jingle all the way,
"Registers are ringing as we near that holiday, hey.
"Jingle bells, jingle bells, jingle all the way,
"Soon the season's over, and that's when we shall pay.

"Dashing through the mall, credit cards held high,
"Oh what fun it is to buy and buy and buy and buy.
"Shopping down one side, and then the upper deck,
"Looking for that special gift, oh well, what the heck.

"Now my arms are full, the lampshade is bent,
"Off to try and find the car, and there's another dent.
"The shopping now is done, the money is all spent,
"Oh my God, what do I do, I didn't pay the rent."

But it doesn't get any better after Christmas.

In a way, I feel sorry for Dec. 26. For at least a month now people have been doing Christmas stuff, like going into debt and grimacing when they open Christmas cards from people to whom they did not send one but should have, and generally being full of joy and good will.

But all that ended yesterday.

Take Christmas trees, for example.

A week or so ago many of us went forth and spent a lot of money buying a cut-down tree. It was a truly gala affair, the whole family doing their Currier and Ives best to have a good time. All that was missing was a sleigh and snow, although in Raleigh we did have some awfully nice mud.

At our house, we got some good friends together, there was a roaring fire in the fireplace, music playing and a splendid time was had by all as we decorated our tree.

Since the tree went up, every eye in the house has constantly looked for burned-out bulbs, the Christmas sin of sins. One non-twinkler and the place became an army camp on alert.

"You go get the bulbs and I'll stay here and watch this one so we can find it again," the orders flew. This is serious stuff and not a moment can be lost. Bulb buyers sallied forth on miserable nights, racing other hastily dispatched bulb buyers to the drug store to pick up new ones.

And when you got there you were forced to paw through nothing but yellow and purple lights, looking for that magical box of mixed colors.

"Daddy, please don't buy red ones, we already have too many red ones now," is a phrase that seems to stick in my mind.

Bulbs bought, we hurried home to make that tree whole again.

But today?

"Hey, Dad, the dog is eating the tree," comes the lackluster alarm.

"So what, it's after Christmas. We'll be taking it down in a couple of days anyway," Dad replies, not really giving a flying flip if that $20 hunk of rapidly drying needles makes it through the hour.

So the tree sits there, bulbs winking out regularly and no one caring. By the time it comes down, at most 30 percent of the bulbs will be burning and everyone will stand around saying what a lovely tree it used to be and complaining about the needles which will remain imbedded in the carpet until near Easter.

And under the withering tree, in that hallowed spot where just yesterday a year's worth of mortgage payments lay disguised as Christmas presents, nothing is left now but a double handful of aluminum foil icicles, three ornaments without hooks, a pair of socks that no one will claim, an unrecognizable part of some very expensive gift, and two misplaced stick-on bows.

The Christmas ham looks like it was run over by a tractor (but is a lot healthier than the checkbook) and everyone is, quite frankly, a little tired of the whole thing.

There are games that no one wants to play, toys that are already broken, the Christmas puppy has messed up the rug eight times already, and the spirit of Christmas has faded in the land.

But look on the bright side. No longer will you have to say to occasional acquaintances, "You ready for Christmas?" or, alternately, "Got your shopping all done?" and then standing there listening to them either brag or complain. You never really did care that much, but last week that was the thing to say.

And the answers, by the way, were invariably, "Lord, no" and "Lord, no."

Now it ends, but remember this, there are only 312 shopping days left until Christmas.

Got your shopping done yet?

Mothers.

Do you understand them?

I don't.

Superman is easy to figure out. He came from Outer Space and that accounts for his amazing strength.

But mothers are from Earth. How can a mother, weighing in at a fast 108 pounds and too weak to take out a 15-

pound bag of garbage, grab a bottle of syrup that has been hiding in the back of the cabinet so long the sticky stuff around the top has turned into tempered steel — and then open it with one twist?

And Superman has great hearing, as you might expect from a space traveler, but mothers?

How can a mother, sound asleep at 2 a.m., with every door in the house closed, hear you when you cough once?

Don't ask me. I don't understand mothers.

Superman can see through walls. Sounds like a nifty trick, right?

Any mother can do that with one eye closed. Just go behind a closed door and do something you ought not to do, like play with the ball in the back of the toilet. Mother's at work, you think, and all is safe.

At that moment the telephone will ring and a cheery voice will ask, "What are you doing?"

How did she know?

Superman is brave, but next to your garden-variety mother he is a 98-pound weakling. At one moment a mother will be cringing in the kitchen from the sight of a tiny bug in the beans. But let a big, ugly, starved, kid-eating monster of a dog come in your yard and even look like he might consider a little leg-nibbling, and the screen door will fly open, a howling banshee will come screaming out of the house and attack the beast with nothing but a flimsy yardstick.

The deed done and the kid saved, the mother will calmly walk back in the house and screech at the sight of a wasp batting itself crazy on the windowpane.

I don't understand mothers.

Mental telepathy is a snap for a card-carrying mother. I defy you to leave your house on a date and spend the next little while at Lover's Lane. Then come home and face your mother.

She knows. And you know she knows. And she knows you know she knows.

And another thing. Mothers never eat.

Let the bills mount up and Mother will take a nip and a tuck in the food budget. But you'll never know it.

Come supper time you'll sit down to a normal meal, but she isn't hungry. She claims she "tasted" while she was cooking and really isn't hungry. But you know better. You know she hasn't eaten a thing. Then why isn't she hungry?

And where do they get all that money? Do they counterfeit quarters? Then how do they always have a spare quarter for a desperate kid whose friends at that very moment are on their way to the store without him?

Few mothers ever attend medical school. But they practice medicine daily. And there is a big difference: Their medicine works.

A mother can take one look at a crushed knee, dust it off and plant a kiss on your grimy forehead. Miraculously the pain goes away, and you watch as the horribly mangled knee becomes a mild scrape and you live to run and walk again. Let's see Marcus Welby do that.

How does she do it?

How does she know when absolutely everything went wrong in school and that big kid beat you up on the way home and you have decided that the only way to preserve your tarnished honor is to run away? And you haven't told a soul?

Is it just chance that on that very day you planned to skip town, she fixes your favorite meal?

Of course not. The only possible explanation is that at the moment of childbirth, when the pain is most intense, God whispers The Secret in her ear.

Tell your Mother you love her this Mother's Day. She'll hear you, no matter where you are or where she is.

She's a mother and she'll know.

The four most despised words in the American tongue are not, as many might expect, the insipid "Have a nice day," although they are truly awful in their own right.

They seem to capture the essence of all that is plastic and meaningless. They are automatic, unfeeling sentiment. When I have been scalped at the gas pump or the check-out line, I do not want the clerk to rub it in with a mandated "Have a nice day."

Why should I have a nice day? They have all my money.

But we stray from the point. The point is there are four words even more irritating.

"Go ask your father."

It is the maternal cop-out of the ages, buck-passing elevated to an art form. I'm sure when Cain picked up that rock and asked Eve if it was all right to bash in Abel's noggin, she said, "Go ask your father."

Much is implied in those four words: Father has all the answers; I wouldn't touch that one on a dare so let's see how the Old Man handles it; go away, kid, you bother me.

I hate to burst the bubble here in the afterglow of Father's Day, but fathers don't always know best. Some fathers barely know enough to come in out of the rain.

"Mom, my bike's busted," comes the plaintive wail.

"Go ask your father," she says.

There are those of us in fatherhood who would injure someone if we grasped a wrench in a public area. We are not all the fathers of TV commercials. I would desert my family for a topless go-go dancer if I ever received a tool on Father's Day.

Because as sure as I got a tool, I would try and do the fatherly thing and use that sucker, and there should be a law against me and tools ever being in the same room together.

"Mom, I've decided to run away from home and become a rock 'n' roll groupie, traveling all over the country in the company of long-haired, speed-eating, hotel-trashing musicians. Is it all right with you?" the kid asks.

"Go ask your father."

Even if we fathers try to turn the tables on the Old Lady, we get caught.

"Dad, if two congruent angles are opposed by three trigometric, non-functioning electrodes, is the geometric equivalent equal to the sum of all the adjacent line segments?"

We'll fix her this time, we think: "Go ask your mother."

"I already did, she said to ask you."

Kids are not stupid ... some of the time. Some of the time kids are amazingly dumb. They can be conned in the blink of an eye. But sometimes their tiny, evil little minds work well.

What the kid does is hang around the kitchen endlessly, boring the socks off dear old Mom with the most incredible string of dull anecdotes from the exciting world of Typing II.

This goes on for hours and finally the kid drops in the biggie, "Mom, can I spend the night at Judy's house?"

The kid's name, of course, is George, but Mom's mind is so numbed out she has not grasped the legal and moral implications of the question. She responds automatically, "Go ask your father."

"Dad, can I spend the night with a friend," George asks, while Dad is watching Walter Cronkite and worried sick about the fluctuations of the Japanese yen. Fathers who watch Walter Cronkite learn a lot about things like that.

"Go ask your mother."

"I did, she said it was all right with her, but to ask you."

"Yeah, go ahead," Dad mutters, figuring that Mom has all the details. The con has worked ... and it is Mom's fault.

Fathers, it is time we cast off the shackles. If you have a wife who is a scientific whiz, the kind of woman who built a nuclear reactor for her ninth-grade science fair, do not fake it through your kid's senior biology homework.

But be a bigger man than they are, so to speak. When the kid hits you with a biggie, don't say, "Go ask your mother."

Instead, say, "Kid, I'm stupid, your mother is brilliant. Get out of here before I sell you to the Arabs for a barrel of oil."

Do not smile gratefully when they hand you a set of screwdrivers on Father's Day, so glad they remembered this special day of days. Pick up one of the screwdrivers and use it to stir your coffee. Make them exchange it for a Linda Ronstadt poster.

When Mom says, "Go ask your father," no matter what the question — be it, "Can I get pregnant for a science project?" or "Can I shoot my sister?" or "Would you like fried puppy for dinner?" — you always give the same answer.

Just say yes to everything. They'll get the idea.

It Ain't Easy

January 15, 1979

The item was buried way down in a story headlined, "Highlights of report on smoking, health."

Paragraph 13 said simply, "Nine out of 10 current smokers have either tried to quit or probably would if they could find an effective way to do it."

And therein lies the problem.

The feds say smoking will kill you. The tobacco folks say, no it won't, either. No one has suggested, however, that smoking is good for you.

I am a confirmed smoker. I have been smoking regularly for almost 20 years. Averaging a pack a day, that comes to something like 146,000 cigarettes up in smoke, roughly 12 miles of cigarettes laid end to end. And I have enjoyed each and every one of them.

For the past 15 years various programs have tried to convince me and my fellow puffers that we should stop smoking. But not once have they come up with a good way to do it.

And until they do, all the scary propaganda in the world won't amount to a puff of smoke.

The first thing that must be dealt with is simple: We enjoy smoking.

It may come as something of a shock to rabid non-smokers, but cigarettes taste good. That's right, the little fellows are downright tasty sometimes. I know some people think the odor of burning tobacco is enough to peel paint, but they aren't trying it from our side of the fire. Nothing, no exquisite French pastry or Mama's banana pudding, ever tasted as good as a cigarette after a big meal.

Then there are the fanatics, the naggers and the do-gooders who want to change the world to their own specifications, which do not include smokers.

As a smoker, I think I speak for all of us when I say, please knock it off.

No smoker I know has even attempted to quit because someone nagged him or her to do so.

We smokers have been cursed, legislated against, left

off party invitations, sneered at, moved away from and had insulting signs posted about us, all by people who think they are doing us a favor. They aren't.

Another story I read last week said that support groups for those trying to quit are ineffective; tapering off is worthless; and about the only way to quit is to simply put the cigarettes down and don't light up again.

But it is absolutely awful to walk up to a guy and say, "How'd you quit?" only to be told, "It was easy, I just stopped one day and I never wanted another cigarette again ever."

I will maliciously run over the next person who says that to me. To a worried smoker thinking about quitting, it is terribly depressing because most of us have secretly tried to quit and have suffered mightily. What people don't understand is that we confirmed smokers are addicted, physically, emotionally and mentally.

I was in surgery one time. I did not have oxygen in my mask. I had essence of Lucky Strike. I survived quite nicely.

Once I quit for close to six weeks. I did not feel better. I felt terrible. I wanted a cigarette every waking moment for six weeks. I was nervous, irritable. I kicked innocent puppies and darling kitties, punched out children and coped not at all well with various crises.

My mind says "Quit, you fool." My body says "No way, sucker."

Do not suggest those filters that take eight weeks. I tried them. I looked like an extra in a 1938 B-grade movie.

Do not suggest smoking only in one place, say a straight-backed chair behind the washing machine. In 24 hours I would have a cot, a refrigerator and the television back there with me.

Do not suggest support groups. Who wants to be in a room with a bunch of wild-eyed people who are on the verge of screaming?

What should be going on is simple. No, Smokin' Joe Califano should not spend a bunch of dollars trying to prove that smoking is harmful. Our mothers knew that as they tanned our rebellious hides when we came home reeking of the devil weed more than two decades ago.

What he should do is find a way to make quitting, if not easy, at least less difficult.

But until he does, there ain't no way but cold turkey, friends, so that's what I'm doing.

So the next time you see me, don't make any loud noises, do not ask me how I feel, do not offer me a cigarette, do not wish me luck, do not discuss it at all. In fact, maybe you shouldn't even get near me.

I will not be fit company for man, woman or child for the next year or so.

January 22, 1979

I didn't know they made weeks as long as the one that just ended.

Is it really only seven days since I swore off the killer weed? Seems longer, somehow, much longer.

I still don't know why I did it. My motivation for setting myself up for the stop-smoking double whammy — misery if I succeeded and public ridicule if I failed — must lie somewhere deep in my psyche.

Tell me, Dr. Freud, why do I put myself in these no-win situations?

But the die is cast. I have publicly stated that I am quitting smoking and I must pay the price, I suppose, including twitching, pacing, snarling and otherwise being my normal, lovable self.

It began, in case you missed it, a week ago when in a fit of mid-winter madness I wrote a column pleading for understanding for smokers.

It is not enough to tell us cigarettes are bad for us, I whined, what you must do is tell us how to quit without pain and suffering. The flesh is weak and the lure of the weed is strong, I opined, so stop yelling and help.

And way down at the bottom of the column I said the only way to quit was cold turkey and that's what I was going to do.

I did not consciously write those words. I was slaving away over my computer terminal and suddenly they appeared as if a friendly gnome had snuck in and written them for me.

But why not, I reasoned, and thus was my life changed.

That was on a Friday. I knew the column would run Monday, thereby giving me a final smoke-filled weekend or two days head start, whichever I chose.

Sometimes I disgust myself. Rather than going for a marathon smoke-in, I chose the head start.

How do you measure success? Normally, I would smoke a pack to a pack and a half of low tar and nicotine cigarettes a day, from say 9 a.m. to midnight. More on weekends and at parties.

On Friday, I smoked three, one in the afternoon when it was either that or hit the boss, one after a dinner you wouldn't believe and one just before turning in when I was too tired to fight it anymore.

Saturday was better. I held myself to two cigarettes and made it until late afternoon before succumbing to the urge.

I was wonderful Sunday. I went to a smoking friend's house where there was a party of sorts under way and smoked only one.

The column ran Monday. I woke up feeling danged near cocky that morning. I was telling the world I was quitting and boy, was I ready.

Then the telephone rang and this thing started getting out of hand. Some woman on the phone — don't ask me who since I remember nothing I'm told until after shaving — told me how wonderful I was to do it and how I'd better not let her down since I had inspired her to quit.

Then some guy on the radio mentioned it, and so even people who can't read knew about it. I got nervous. I have weird visions of breaking under the strain and rushing into a store to buy cigarettes, only to have the clerk point at me and scream, "Here he is, the traitor, stone him, stone him." Then all the people in the store would gather around and hurl hard things at me.

You think about things like that when you're quitting. That's what breathing fresh air does to your brain.

But I hung in there Monday. Late that night I ran into a

long-absent friend, and, before I knew it, she had handed me a cigarette, and I was halfway through it. But I didn't finish it.

Tuesday I was completely smoke free. Wednesday I faltered just at the beginning of the Carolina-State game and had one. Thursday I was clean again.

The tally: during the past week I probably would have smoked about 250 cigarettes. I smoked eight.

I also have yelled at people I shouldn't yell at, thought about smoking a lot, thoroughly enjoyed those eight cigarettes I did smoke, walked around my office and home for mile after endless mile.

I also have not taken 20 minutes to get my lungs going in the morning.

It is not easy, but it is possible ... I think.

My boss tells me I'm prolonging the agony by slipping even once. Possibly that is true, but in my case it is easier to give in a little when the going gets really tough than to set impossible goals and then get disheartened when you fail.

When you're trying to quit, disheartened is the last thing you need to be.

And when I finally get this thing under control and proclaim myself a non-smoker, I'd better not get run over by a truck.

That wouldn't be fair at all.

March 15, 1979

I didn't make it.

Front Porches
And Back Roads

Macon.

One of the things I like most about small towns is that they're usually pretty quiet. So I was expecting little more than a quiet visit and a cold drink when I pulled into Haithcocks Store here on N.C. 158 in Warren County.

It is amazing how wrong I can be sometimes. I should have gone to Times Square if I was looking for peace and quiet. Macon was jumping.

"Hello, you want to be blown up?" Charlie Haithcock asked me when I walked in.

"Well, no, I hadn't planned on it," I answered, mentally deciding I still had plenty of time to make it to the door. "What do you have in mind?"

"We had us a bomb threat today," he said. "Man called and said the place was going to blow up at six o'clock tonight. A deputy came here when we called him and he said there probably wasn't much to worry about. I hope he's right."

"I hope so, too," I answered, checking out the route to the door one more time, just in case. "I tell you what. I'll go on down the road a bit and write about it if it does blow up."

As you can see, I think pretty fast on my feet.

Charlie didn't seem too worried about it, and neither

38

did Mrs. Irene Duncan, the feisty lady behind the cash register.

"I'm not worried about it at all," she said. "Of course, I get off at three o'clock but I promised them I'd listen real good to see if the place blew up."

And then L.M. Haithcock Jr., known as Junior, came in. I asked him how he felt about the situation. I pointed out there could be a bomb right under where we were standing.

"You'd better shut down for 30 minutes," he cautioned. "If you folks get blown up I'd have to work 17 hours a day every day instead of 17 hours every other day. You can do what you want, though, 'cause I ain't going to be here."

I asked him where he was off to, other than out of bomb range.

"We're going up to look for that body in Lake Gaston," he said.

A body? First a bomb and now a body? I started easing my way toward the door.

"Yeah, they think there's a body in Lake Gaston," he said. "There is supposed to have been a murder somewhere and they think the body is in the lake. We're going to drag for it if we can get a boat in. I was down there a while ago and I drove my truck out on the ice, so we'll have to find somewhere else to put the boat in, I reckon."

Haithcock's Store is one of those places you don't see much of anymore, the kind of place that sells anything.

The senior L. M. Haithcock bragged, "I bet you won't find another place that has a Grade A meat market and a Grade A worm market in the same building."

I told him I hoped I wouldn't and then asked Mrs. Duncan if there was anything they didn't have.

"If we don't have it, we're expecting a load of it tomorrow," she said.

And, by the way, the place didn't blow up.

Rountree.

The combined age of the men at the card table was 254 years, most of those years spent playing the game called "set back."

I hope you know how to play because I sure can't tell you. I stood and watched Johnny Craft, Noble Craft, Bruce Manning and Perry McLawhon play for the better part of two hours and, while it looks like fun, all I could figure out was that it involves trumps, slapping the table, bidding and picking on one another.

Such as:

Noble: "When I win it's a game of skill. When they win it's pure luck."

Perry: "Those boys don't work 'cause they're sorry. I don't work because I'm retired."

Noble: "Bruce gets a little cocky when he starts winning and Johnny gets red in the face when he loses, so we have to let up on him some."

This crew has been together for a long time. Noble and Johnny are brothers and everybody else seems to be related in some fashion. Noble and Bruce are cousins who still live within 200 yards of each other as they have since they were boys together 50 or 60 years ago.

After a lifetime of farming they have the time now to sit around sister Phoebe Carman's crossroads store and play some set back.

"I reckon we play the same rules as everyone else," Noble said. "Our fathers taught us to play and we play just like they did.

"And we don't cheat or have signals and like that. But, yes, we're pretty good set back players, I reckon."

The set back tradition of Roundtree will go on. When I went in Noble was holding his eight-month-old grandson Bryan in one arm and dealing with the other. And then Bryan's father Terry came by to eat some ice cream and play a few hands. And sister Phoebe sits in from time to time.

The place where they play has been a crossroads store for a century or so; no one can remember when it wasn't there at the corner of N. C. 102 and an unnamed county road near Ayden in Pitt County.

Phoebe's husband Willis ran it for 40 years and when he died three years ago Phoebe just kept coming to work every day.

"These boys have been a lifesaver to me," she said, between selling drinks and crackers to the farm workers who came to the dark, air-conditioned barn of a store. "They got to coming up here to be with me and started playing set back while they sat here. Now they play about all the time."

This is family, and a close knit one, but outsiders are welcome to sit in. I chose not to; there are enough ways to make a fool out of myself without playing a game I don't understand.

They'd even like to play folks at other crossroads sometimes. They've heard there is a crowd up in Wilton that thinks they are pretty good and the folks from Roundtree would love to take them on, or anyone else who is interested.

"You make sure you write that we'd be proud to play anybody, but we don't cheat," Noble said.

Jamesville.

Gene Williams slapped his ample stomach with a hand the size of an expensive steak and took another healthy slug of beer he held casually in the other hand.

"It takes a month to get the scent off of me," he said, rubbing that tan and glistening expanse while an Easter Monday sun broiled down as if to say, "Hey, remember me?"

It has been, by all accounts, a thoroughly rotten winter, so it is understandable if the rivermen of Jamesville threw themselves into this year's annual herring run with an extra helping of good old boy gusto.

"I sometimes take as much as three or four weeks vacation while the herring are running," Williams said. "Just yesterday I started fishing at five in the morning and I didn't leave till midnight."

Three feet away, flat-bottomed boats piled high with nets gave forth with this year's catch of herring, shad and rockfish. The fast-running Roanoke River was alive with boats and nets as far up or down the river as you could see.

The herring start running early in the spring, urged on

their way by a silent signal only they seem to hear. They come back from the sea to swim up the Roanoke to where they themselves were spawned.

For longer than anyone can remember, the men of Jamesville have gathered by the river this time of year, hauling their loaded nets into small boats, ripping the yellow-red roe from the bellies of swollen fish, selling some, eating a lot, giving some away, drinking beer, swapping lies and generally rejoicing in the sure knowledge that no matter what else happens, the herring always come back.

And so do Jamesville's sons and daughters.

"Easter weekend has become a family reunion in Jamesville," Mrs. Joyce Paduch said as she took a break from selling hot dogs in the rescue squad trailer. "Over the years it has developed that Easter weekend, when it doesn't come too late, is about at the height of the herring run and it has become a tradition for everyone to come home that weekend. It is a community party."

To celebrate this renewal of life in the Roanoke, the river people gather by the water's edge where simple shacks — like the Sugar Shack or the Green Leaf Motel — hang precariously over the water.

"There was a time when I could dress 50 herring in one minute," Bill Perry, who with Williams owns the Green Leaf, said while his hands performed lightning-quick surgery on the fish in front of him.

One slice through the body and then turn the blade along the soft underside, raking the roe out with one motion, makes it look simple. It isn't.

Down at the Sugar Shack, Ronnie Modlin was almost sold out, leaving him plenty of time to smile about the 21-pound rockfish he'd caught and now had proudly on display in his cooler. Boys with fertilizer company hats gawked in appropriate awe. It was a monster.

"It's better this year," 68-year-old Bryant Reason said. "Those Russians used to get all the herring and for a couple of years it was poor fishing. But I've seen the time when the river was black with the small fish going downstream after they were hatched.

"But we've had a big run for the last two weeks and people have been coming from all over to catch 'em or buy 'em or eat 'em.

"It'll be all over in another month, but it's a fine time now."

Kelly.

"I like to stepped on the ugly thing," Jimmy Carter said. "Scared me so bad I jumped back.

"He was so ugly and about the size of your fist, I figured he'd die."

But the bird didn't die, and for eight glorious months, the folks in this Bladen County crossroads had themselves a bona-fide legend.

His name was "Nevermore," a shiny black crow that squawked into a community's heart and flew out again just as suddenly.

"I was feeding the hogs one day, and I found him lying on the ground," said Carter, a Kelly farmer. "He must have been 10 or 15 feet from a tree, so I don't know how he got there, he wasn't even old enough to have feathers. Lord, that thing was ugly, sure enough.

"I put him in a box in the garage. I still figured there was no way he could make it and fed him stuff like bread soaked in milk and blueberries. He loved it all, but his favorite was raw hamburger.

"After he feathered out, he was real pretty, all black and shiny. One day in the spring I put him in his box under a tree. There was never a top on that box, he stayed because he wanted to.

"He got to where he could climb up on a limb from his box, but he still couldn't fly or climb back down, so I'd get out the ladder and get that crow out of a tree where he was stuck and hollering for me. Pretty soon he got to where he knew how to climb up and down the ladder, so I just left it by the tree. Only bird I ever saw that used a ladder to get up and down a tree.

"He started learning to fly by himself, jumping off low things and flapping his wings. And pretty soon, he got to where he could do it good. He'd fly a few feet from the box he lived in, but then he'd come back.

"Then he got to where he'd fly around the yard, but he always came back.

"He dearly loved to ride. He'd get in the car every time you opened it up and go anywhere with the windows down.

"I'd be breaking up land with the tractor, and he'd fly from the house down to the field and ride for hours sitting on my shoulder.

"He really loved to go up to Sam Potter's store, and he wasn't afraid of anyone. He'd hop up on their shoulders, pull shiny pens out of their pockets and talk to them. Everybody knew him.

"That crow would fly five miles from here, visiting people, and then he'd fly home for lunch and back out again until suppertime.

"One Sunday morning he went to church, just flew over there, lit on the sidewalk and hopped his way up the stairs just like people.

"The only thing he didn't like was other birds. They used to pick on him, and he was glad to see me when I rescued him.

"He was the talk of Kelly, he'd go to see people and leave when he wanted to do something else. But he never was in a cage or spent more than two nights anywhere but in my garage.

"Then it got to be dove hunting season, and I just knew he'd get killed, so I put him in a cage. Nevermore looked so miserable in that cage that I just had to let him out, whether he got killed or not.

"He loved people, and I knew he'd fly right up to a hunter, and some of those city people will shoot anything that moves when they get a gun in their hands.

"It was the beginning of dove season when a man hunting on my land shot him. Nevermore made it home, and in a week he was doing all right, he wasn't hurt too bad, but that made me so mad, especially since the man had been warned about Nevermore being a pet crow and a fellow was hollering at him not to shoot when he shot him.

"I really laid it on that fellow. I didn't cuss him or hit him, but I laid it on him good.

"Those people from town, you hate to tell them they

can't hunt on your land, but they shoot everything and throw cans in your fields, it's enough to make you sick.

"Nevermore got better in a week and began to fly around the yard. It was the next Sunday after he got shot, in the fall, I reckon, and Sam Potter's boy said he saw him up at the gas pumps about noon.

"That was the last time he was seen in Kelly.

"He was so friendly he could have flown in somebody's car window, and they took him off, or maybe he was killed.

"Personally, I think he was crow-napped.

"Please put in your story that if anybody knows what happened to him, I'd sure appreciate it if they'd let me know.

"I wouldn't never want another one, but he was sure something else."

Louisburg.

"Once she was a normal 16-year-old," the barker insisted. "Now she is a chained animal.

"She is alive and inside. Come see what drugs can do. See Jenny, a living nightmare. It is shocking but true."

All of this was delivered in a high-energy spiel, urging me to step inside the ratty tent and have a peek.

So I did.

I didn't see much. "Jenny" was a rather homely young girl sitting on a quilt on the grass, "chained" by a loop around her ankle large enough to slip on and off with ease, and staring at an orange and white teddy bear.

But I missed the best part. Passing by a few minutes late, I was overrun by a crowd screaming out of Jenny's tent. Seems drug-crazed Jenny had "escaped," only to be caught in the nick of time by her brave owner.

Such is a night at the county fair.

I love fairs. I love to eat greasy onions and peppers on a Polish sausage. I love being badgered by shills for gambling games that would be illegal anywhere but at the fair. I love the lights and the rumble of rides, although I have more sense than to pay someone to spin me in all directions until I'm sick. I love it all, even the canned pickles and knitting.

The Franklin County Fair, unlike some, is not sponsored by a civic organization. It is the private domain of Jolly Bunn, local town commissioner, assistant fire chief, groceryman and for 16 years, fair promoter.

"It's in my blood," Jolly said, sitting regally in front of his trailer office. "I do it because I love it."

Never was a man more aptly named that Jolly Bunn. He is, as they say, a real character.

"I was born on Christmas Day 1931," he said. "My daddy wanted to call me 'Depression' but my mamma said, 'Why he's a jolly little thing' and the name stuck."

This year's production should be preserved in plastic and put in a museum somewhere. If ever a fair was typical of small county fairs in North Carolina, this is it.

From the time you park in the dusty field next door, through the $1-a-head ticket gate, pass the display of National Guard equipment and big tractors, through the display building where 4-H clubs do their best to make us eat right, grow good pastures and take care of our teeth, past the jars of canned food and out onto the midway with those weird people who inhabit traveling carnivals, this one has it all.

Fairs are for kids and the crowd in Louisburg was having quite a time. They rode on everything that moved, begged daddies to make fools of themselves and go broke trying to win teddy bears (which the fathers did willingly), gawked at the ladies outside the girly show and tried to slip in, flirted with the opposite sex, dunked clowns into tanks of water and had a good time.

It can get seedy, as do all fairs, but that is part of the charm. You know good and well you will pay more for prizes than they cost, or else the game booth would go broke. You know that when you put your quarter down on a colored square and wait for the ball to stop rolling, the odds against winning are 16 to 1 — but you do it anyway. That's what you do at fairs.

And you know when you go in the girly show you will see three girls with no looks and less talent do raunchy things, but you go anyway.

I hope county fairs go on forever. Somehow, when the air is cool and the moon is bright and the crops are almost in and school has started and the sun sets earlier, I need to go to a fair.

Bailey.

The next time one of those oft-mentioned late afternoon and evening thundershowers is headed this way, I do not plan to visit Clifton Bissette.

There is no telling what might happen.

This tale goes back to March 1978. It was hot and muggy that early spring day, and no one minded when it clouded up and a good rain came through.

Bissette didn't really mind when he went out to his hog pen and found that a maple tree 2 feet in diameter had been blown over, ripped right out of the ground by the wind that came with the rain.

"I just left it lying there," Bissette said. "It was pretty late in the year, and I had plenty of stove wood, so I figured I'd wait until this fall to cut it up."

Besides, his hogs liked to wallow in the rich, black hole about 12 feet across that was gouged out of the earth when the big tree toppled.

Bissette said the tree lay all summer where it had fallen. Big roots on one side were still attached to the ground, so there was no problem with the tree rolling over and killing a hog or two.

The farm summer slid by in a dusty haze. As he had for the past 65 years, Bissette worked the land, sleeping each night in the house where he was born 71 years ago.

Then came that Sunday afternoon that Bissette and his wife, Etta, will never forget.

"The story has been told all over the county, but I don't think most of 'em believe what happened that day," he said. "But it happened."

It was getting on toward dark that Sunday — Aug. 20, 1978. Mrs. Bissette was away visiting, and Clifton was on the place alone, enjoying his day of rest but keeping a watchful eye on the barn full of tobacco that was curing in the tin-sided log barn that sits right across the path from the hog pen where the maple tree had lain for five months.

It started clouding up that Sunday afternoon, Bissette remembers, promising one of those boisterous thunder-boomers that ruin picnics and make driving hazardous but feel so good when the rain stops and the air is chilly clean.

He said the wind suddenly picked up, dusty leaves on the trees fluttering like frightened birds. The rain came in a rush, hard and fast, spit from a mean sky.

It rained and blew hard for a few minutes, nothing serious, a good dust-settler that farmers love.

And when it was over, Bissette, like any good farmer, walked out to check things over.

He said the first thing he saw was that another tree, a big water oak near the hog pen, had blown over, missing his pen of prized rabbit dogs.

Then the farmer said he saw something he hadn't seen in all his born days — the maple tree was standing upright again.

"I've been around a long time and I ain't never seen the wind blow a tree up," he said. "Now I've seen it blow them down plenty, but never seen one blown up before."

And it stands there yet, straight and tall in the hog pen with not a single dead limb, not even a dead leaf, to show for its up and down summer.

I did not see the tree when it was down, nor was I there when Bissette said the wind blew it back up again. All I saw was the evidence. There is a 12-foot diameter circle of disturbed earth and there is broken brush where the tree lay on its side for a summer.

It is clear from the evidence on Bissette's farm that something very strange happened to that maple, something strange indeed.

The wind that did it had to have blown in exactly the opposite direction from the wind that blew it down, right through the same low place. it could have been a tornado, I suppose, although Bissette says he never heard the tell-tale roar that usually accompanies tornadoes. He just remembers a gusty rain.

But it was powerful, whatever it was. The same wind

roared through a 2-foot square vent in the side of the tobacco barn and blew the cover off his barn burners, something that has not happened in 20 years.

If it ever clouds up when I'm at Bissette's farm, you can bet your "Cat" hat that I'm going to town.

Yeatsville.

There is a sign just to the left as you walk into Wess Windley's store by the highway here that reads:

"We have been in business since February, 1934. We have been pleasing and displeasing the public ever since. We have been cussed and discussed, boycotted, talked about, lied to, hung up, held up and robbed.

"The only reason we are staying in business is to see what in the hell is going to happen next."

Most likely what will happen next, now that the rich Beaufort County earth is warming enough to be worked and the farmers are back at work, is that some fool tourist will drive past on U.S. 264, whip his or her head around, slow down, turn around and come back to look at Wess Windley's gas pump.

They will chat for a moment and then the tourist will shyly ask if he can take a picture. Windley, as he has for thousands of them, will walk out to the pump, put his hand on the lever and pose. Click, just one more, please, click and then they'll drive off, satisfied they have captured another piece of fading Americana.

What's so special about Wess Windley's gas pump? Not much. But when is the last time you saw a hand-operated gas pump? You may remember them, tall, gangly things, with a glass tank on top. Crank the handle back and forth, pump the gas up into the glass tank (measured by the gallon and not the penny), put the nozzle in the tank and let gravity do the rest.

"I got it in 1934 when I opened here," said Windley, a small, devilishly funny and engaging 82-year-old farmer. "The thing was worn out then. We didn't get our electricity here until 1938 and then I got an electric pump, and it's still here, right out there beside the hand one."

The Windleys have been here by the side of the road for

a long time now.

"My great-great-grandfathers came here from England or Ireland — we never did figure out which — as stowaways," Wess chuckled. "They'd probably killed somebody. And I remember my father telling me he used to see the rebels marching past here many times.

"I saw the first automobile go past here myself. It was in 1904 or 1905. John Wilkerson from Belhaven was coming from Washington right down this road in a steamer, either a Stanley or a White. They tell me he got arrested in Washington for going 12 miles an hour. That was speeding. Now you've got to pick your time to cross that road."

The years have taken their toll at Wess Windley's store. For years Mrs. Windley ran the store while Wess did some farming and some carpentry work, but in recent years, since she died and he got a little older, Wess spends most of his days here, chewing the fat with whomever happens by.

"Been many a crop of tobacco harvested here by this old oil stove," he said, grinning. "Many a fish caught and many a building built. Many a lie told, too, most of what's told, as a matter of fact."

Windley has no time for the new trends in merchandising.

"Don't take no credit cards," he said. "Had some trouble with two or three and that was it. You take a bad card and you lose, not Texaco. I might lose a sale now and then, but I might save me some money, too."

About now, you might be thinking Wess Windley and his hand pump are nothing more than a colorful part of the past, an old geezer hanging on for old times sake. But think again.

Quick, if an ice storm knocked out electricity for three days, where would you buy gas?

"We have some bad storms down here sometimes and one time the power was off for three days," Windley said. "I had them stacked up during the gas shortage.

"They tell me I've got the only hand pump in seven counties.

"I had an antique dealer tell me it was worth $1,000. The Texaco people told me I ought to sell.

But he won't.

"Pumping that thing is good exercise, and I'd rather wear out than rust away," he said. Besides, I suspect he'd miss watching the tourists.

Deep Run.

The water lies in mirror-like stillness, reflecting the double image of tall cypress trees.

On a log sit nine ducks, preening themselves in the sleepy summer heat.

Dragon flies, like helicopters on jungle patrol, dart low over the brown-black water.

The periscope-like head of a lazy turtle breaks the surface so smoothly it leaves no ripples, and then goes under to the dark safety of the sandy bottom.

A dragon fly gets careless. Dipping too low, its long body touches the water.

The quick splash comes suddenly, a silver shadow pimples the surface and the dragon fly is gone, a late breakfast for a hungry bass.

On the bank, beneath the towering cypress trees, Christine Stanley hums softly to herself, keeping time with the gentle rhythm of summer songbirds as she shucks fresh corn.

A puppy sleeps safely in the cool, wet sand by her feet.

It is good to be here in the shade.

Christine and Carroll Stanley have lived by the edge of Tull Mill Pond, known as Tull's Mill around here, for 20 years, feeding the ducks, renting boats to fishermen and enjoying the good life.

Four days a week, Carroll is away, working as a crew chief with the State Department of Transportation, clearing ditches and roadsides in Lenoir County.

While he is away, Christine does the work.

"Yeah, when it's time to bail out the boats, Carroll gets gone," she says, the love in her voice shining through.

There is plenty of bailing to do this muggy morning. A heavy rain the night before makes the boats ride low in the water, a sweat-raising job to dip them dry for the fishermen who come to prowl the dark, upper reaches of Tull's Mill.

"Seems like we've been busier this year than ever before," she says. "The spring was so bad the men couldn't wait to go fishing when it got nice."

The puppy stirs now, making friends with a stranger.

"Somebody put her out last week," Christine says. "I don't want her to stay around but I'm afraid to give her away. I'm afraid she wouldn't get a good home."

This is a gentle lady, in a gentle place.

I figured that since Christine gets to spend her days by a favorite fishing hole, she would at least wet a hook from time to time.

"If I get ready to go, seems like everybody else wants to go right then," she said. "I go about twice a year.

"I catch my fish with a silver hook — with money at the fish market."

It is a distinctively country way of doing business here. Jammed in the screen door are several signs: "Gone to Pink Hill," "Gone to Deep Run," "Be back in a few minutes," and one that says simply, "Gone."

"When that one is up, they know I ain't coming back for awhile," she says. "They fish now and pay me later. Not a half a dozen people in 20 years haven't paid."

Carroll once told his wife something that pretty much sums up why they have never left here.

"I've been to California twice," he said. "And I've never seen any place prettier than right here at this pond."

Castoria.

You can say this about Elma Harrell.

He is not a man to waste time. He sees what he wants and it's "katie, bar the door."

Take the case of Mrs. Harrell.

"I was too old to keep waiting," Elma said. "I saw her come up for gas outside. I thought she was a fine looking woman so I asked her to come inside and talk for awhile.

"And then I found out she was a widow woman."

That did it. The gas pump scene happened just over a year ago and next month the couple will celebrate their first wedding anniversary.

"I'll be 64 years old this summer and I didn't want to wait any longer," Elma said. "And now we've had 12 months together and it's been just fine."

I should say so. If I had a raven-haired beauty like Jennie Harrell to bring me a big plate of collards, a ham hock the size of a baseball, a mess of peas and a quart jar full of dark iced tea, I'd be doing fine, too.

That's what Elma was packing away for lunch the other day when I stopped by the Castoria Country Store to get a cold drink and some crackers.

Don't bother to look for Castoria on the map. About the only way to find it is to drive south from Walstonburg on N. C. 91. You'll find it about halfway to Snow Hill.

Elma works part-time at the store and the day I was by he was doing a brisk business in sardines, crackers, Co' Colas, Vienna sausage, potted meat and pork and beans.

It was tobacco-setting time in Green County and the working folks were hungry.

"I worked on a farm for most of my life and it's hard work all right," Elma said, reared back behind his counter while Jennie perched nearby keeping an eye on him. "But you can say one thing about it. You can get a day off to go fishing when you want to.

"In a store you don't have time for such as that."

Jennie is taking things a little easier these days too.

She ran a soda shop in nearby Maury for 26 years until she quit to marry Elma. Now she does a little clerking in post offices around and takes care of Elma.

Not that Elma needs much taking care of. He's 63, going on 50.

"I've worked as hard as the next man, I reckon," Elma said. "I was head of a family when I was 16 and I worked, but I took pretty good care of myself, didn't I?"

The newlyweds took themselves a trip not long ago. They went up north so Elma could show Jennie off to some relatives.

"It was my first plane trip," Elma said. "And then in Washington I stood there and watched them work on it for two hours. I figured if the bailing wire held out we'd make it home all right.

"Then I got home and read about all them plane crashes.

"And that was my last flight."

Explain your first name, I said. Elmo I've heard and Elmers are common enough, but Elma?"

"I don't know," Elma said. "I had a first grade teacher and she taught me to spell it 'E-l-m-a.'

"They weren't keeping birth certificates then, so I stuck with Elma. But I did name my son Elmer."

Love is supposed to be something that only young people understand. But while they court by telephone and on skateboards and at the movies, it's refreshing to see a country man and his country wife sit there holding hands at the crossroads store.

Ain't love grand?

Echoes

Some things you don't see much anymore, things you wonder whatever happened to, some things you might never have seen and some things to remember:

Big trees in the front yard with their trunks painted white.

Green front-porch swings.

Polka music on the radio.

A lazy dog, sleeping in the middle of a dirt street.

Flypaper, the kind that was yellow-brown and hung in a long sticky curl.

The slam of a screen door with a new spring.

Thermometers advertising Tru-Ade Orange drink.

Rings for shooting marbles drawn in the dirt.

Postcards that say "Wish you were here."

Kids dusting erasers on the back wall of a school house.

Jawbreakers.

"See Rock City" signs painted on the sides of barns.

A plastic statue of Jesus stuck on the dashboard of a car.

Popcorn boxes folded flat and sailed like Frisbees during afternoon wars at the Saturday matinee.

Wax lips.

A back porch with a pump and a nail to hang a towel.

The sound of a mother calling her child at dusk on a still summer evening, the sound wafting for miles.

Kids playing, "One, two, three, redlight" or "May I."

Women using parasols.
Eastern North Carolina's legendary Goat Man.
Funeral home fans.
Mud flaps and handlebar streamers on bicycles.
A kid riding off to adventure on a broomstick horse.
Sweetheart chairs in soda fountains.
Those little white bags of powder used to keep white buck shoes Pat Boone-fresh.
Fender skirts.
Red Ryder and L'il Beaver.
DC-3 airplanes.
Love beads.
Soda straw containers that looked like big glass jars with a shiny metal lid that you raised and pulled all the straws up at once.
Leon Errol.
White-painted tires used as planters.
Hopscotch squares drawn on a sidewalk with chalk.
Washbasins.
Fox furs, complete with heads, feet and tails.
Cuspidors.
Metal six-pack cartons for soft drinks.
Beanies.
Bronzed baby shoes made into lamps or clocks.
Donald Duck bicycles with a horn in his mouth and lights in his eyes.
Old men and young boys listening to ball games on a front porch.
Penny loafers with pennies.
Pea shooters.
Cowboys with two guns.
Little wax bottles filled with flavored water that you drank and then ate the wax.
Motorcycle hats, the kind worn by Marlon Brando in "The Wild One."
Leather flaps and huge tongs, the kind every ice man used.
Playing cards clipped to bicycle fenders with closepins. Brrrrrr.
Spinner hubcaps.
A woman in a hat and white gloves.
Sun visors on the outside of car windshields.
Three-color sheets of plastic stuck to the front of black

and white TV sets to make them look like color.
Fuzzy dice hanging from a rearview mirror.
Scarecrows.
An old man driving a mule and wagon down a country road.
Tire swings.
Davy Crockett coonskin caps.
"Kilroy was here" graffiti.

By the Hand of God

Swan Quarter.

This is a weird story and you can believe it or not.

That's up to you. But there are a lot of people and legal documents that say it really happened this way.

The year was 1874 and the Methodists here had decided it was time they had themselves a church.

Wanting to build on the highest ground in this low-lying Hyde County town, they went to see Sam Sadler, a prosperous landowner, about a lot he had.

It was prime real estate and Sam was smart. He told them there was no way he would give it away, and furthermore, don't even bother to ask again.

So they gave up and went to work building their simple frame church on land they got from H. A. Hayes. It was a nice lot, but dangerously close to sea level.

The church was dedicated on Sept. 16, 1876, and it was a joyous Sunday. The Methodists finally had themselves a church.

Three days later a storm roared into Swan Quarter.

All day Wednesday it rained and the wind howled. Wednesday night saw flooding and roofs ripped from homes. Some houses were destroyed by the rampaging weather.

The storm continued into Thursday when it finally began to wane.

Water stood five feet deep in places and Swan Quarter was a devastated town.

Suddenly someone looked at the humble little Methodist Church. The force of the water had moved it from its spindly brick pilings and it was floating into the street, a street now called Oyster Creek Road.

It moved slowly up the street in spite of everything the men could do to stop it. It bumped into a general store located about where the Swan Quarter Volunteer Fire Department sits now.

Men tied ropes to the building, fighting for a footing in the swirling water but they couldn't hold it. It kept moving until it reached the center of town, the corner of Oyster Creek Road and U. S. 264 Business.

Then a curious thing happened.

The building took a sharp right turn and headed down that road like some giant living thing.

It went for two more blocks that way, men fighting to hold it back, until it reached the corner of what is now Church Street.

Then it moved slightly off its straight-line course and settled to the ground as the water receded.

It stopped right in the middle of the lot Sam Sadler had refused to sell, the exact place the Methodists had wanted their church in the first place.

The next morning Sam went to the courthouse and gave the land to Methodists.

Like I said, you can believe it or not, but the people here do, people like the Rev. Robert F. Randalls, the former pastor, who told me the story of Providence United Methodist Church.

"Every time I researched the story and got another little piece of information, a chill ran up my back," the preacher said.

"I talked to old people who had seen it and one thing is certain. That building moved in spite of everything people could do."

On the front of the small building, located just behind the new Methodist Church, is a small sign that says simply, "The church moved by the hand of God."

You can argue with that if you want to.

I won't.

The Lovers

Beaufort.

He was a promising young man, soon to be a Philadelphia lawyer in the days when that meant something.

She was a Southern belle, the beautiful 16-year-old daughter of the town doctor.

He was Charles French. She was Nancy Manney. The year was 1836. And the story, says Beaufort author Mary Paul who graciously allowed me to use it, is true.

Charles met Nancy in 1836 when he was hired by Dr. Manney to tutor Nancy and her brothers and sisters. Charles had been a law student in Philadelphia, but the chance of spending two years in the romantic seaport of Beaufort was a compelling lure.

For two years, Charles taught the Manney children by day and fell in love with Nancy by night. It was their secret, a genteel love affair between teacher and pupil.

The time soon came for Charles to leave Beaufort and return to school. He approached Dr. Manney, confessed his love for Nancy and asked permission to return after his graduation and claim her as his bride.

But the wise, old doctor had known what was going on, and he did not approve. Charles could not marry Nancy now or later. The relationship was to end, and Charles was never to return.

But young love, while often foolish, is nonetheless strong. The young couple swore their love would not die and promised to write each other until the day Charles would return and marry Nancy.

But Dr. Manney was resolute in his opposition. Angered and grief-stricken that his daughter would defy him, the doctor met with the town postmaster, and it was agreed that letters between the star-crossed lovers would not be delivered. Nancy's letters would not leave Beaufort. Charles's letters would never reach Nancy.

Nancy wrote almost daily, pledging her love for Charles and telling him of her daily life in the village by the sea. But the letters never left the post office. They were collected, tied in a bundle and never forwarded.

Charles wrote as well. His letters came to the post office in Beaufort where they joined the growing pile of letters from Nancy.

The years drifted by in a lonely parade of days. Nancy never quit writing, although she never received an answer. Dr. Manney died, never telling Nancy of his secret pact with the postmaster.

The Civil War came to the South. Nancy by this time was approaching middle age. She had never married. She lived a lonely, troubled life, but her love for Charles never wavered, never faded. She remained true to him.

When she was 45, the terrible secret was told to her. The postmaster, on his death bed, feeling guilty and wanting to die in peace, called Nancy to his bedside and handed her the bundle of letters, the written remnants of a love that was doomed.

Charles's letters had stopped coming years ago. He assumed that because he had not heard from her, she had found another.

She was sure he had married. It was over. She knew it, although she still loved Charles. She spent the next few years helping tend to the Civil War wounded.

In 1885, Nancy was summoned to the post office. There was a letter there, asking for information about the Manney family. The writer said he had known the family years before and was planning a visit if any of the Manney family still lived in Beaufort. It was signed by the chief justice of the Arizona Territory Supreme Court. It bore the signature of Charles French.

Nancy Manney was now 65. She hurriedly wrote Charles telling him to come to Beaufort. She loved him still.

She was also dying.

Friends met the chief justice when his ship slipped into Beaufort. He was an old man, dignified, eager to see his lovely Nancy. His wife, whom he had married after no letters from Nancy arrived, had died years before, and he was alone.

Nancy did not meet Charles at the ship. She was too sick to leave her bed.

Finally the lovers met, she in bed and he by her side.

The room was filled with roses; he had told her years before that she reminded him of roses. It was a bittersweet reunion and once again Charles French asked Nancy Manney to be his bride.

She said "yes," and on their wedding day the aging Charles French knelt by Nancy Manney's bed, lifted the sick old woman in his arms and they were wed.

A few days later, Nancy Manney died.

1956-1960

Wilson.

The 1950s, if you believe television, were an endless string of "Happy Days."

Those of us lucky enough to have grown up in that fun-filled era all had dates every weekend, a souped-up car, wore neato ducktail haircuts and had friends with nicknames like Fonzie and Potzie.

I don't know about you, but it wasn't exactly like that for those of us who went to dear old Ralph L. Fike Senior High School, class of 1960.

We did have a guy in our school who rode a motorcycle of sorts, like that Fonzie person on TV, but his name was Melvin, he drove an Italian scooter and he made good grades in chemistry.

Melvin had pimples, crooked teeth, wore a gray jacket from a double-breasted gabardine suit and had his first date when he was 26 and in Tijuana, Mexico, on leave from the Navy.

But we had dances, by gosh. Hundreds of dances. Everytime we turned around someone was holding a dance in the lunchroom. And they were always the same.

The first to arrive were the sponsors, usually from the Future Car Washers of America or the Algebra Club. They would mix up a batch of red stuff and pour it into 12,000 tiny little cups which were tastefully arranged on the table borrowed from the Industrial Arts class. A thin film of sawdust spread quickly on the red stuff, but nobody cared. We wouldn't have drunk that stuff on a dare.

Then the crowd would arrive. The young gentlemen stood on one side of the room and talked about the young ladies standing on the other side. We told jokes, punched each other's shoulders (mostly I got my shoulder punched), said awful things about the girls and claimed we were having loads of fun.

Everyone, that is, except Millard.

Millard was cool. He wore a white London Fog windbreaker with the collar turned up, a faded madras plaid shirt, a pair of black pants pegged to 13 inches, white socks, black loafers and enough oil on his hair to solve the energy crisis.

Millard would cut a girl from the pack and they would stand in the middle of the floor, holding tightly to each other and move each foot exactly one inch each 35 seconds. It didn't matter how fast or dreamy (we didn't have slow songs, we had dreamy songs) the songs were, Ole Millard and his lady never changed their shuffle.

The rest of us stood on our side of the room, brazenly trying to decide which girl was worthy of our attention. We usually brazenly stood there until the dance was over.

But occasionally one of us would get up enough nerve to walk across the room, ask a girl to dance and get turned down. A rejection like that, with all your friends watching, made that long walk back across the lunchroom about as much fun as taking your shoes off at the shoe store and finding a hole in your sock.

Then we'd all go to a drive-in — and until you've walked to a drive-in, you don't know the meaning of shame — and stand around bragging that a girl had blown in your ear right there in the lunchroom.

And that's why I love "Happy Days" on the tube. I always was a fan of science-fiction.

Before Kitty Hawk

Belhaven.

The year was 1889 and the folks who knew 14-year-old John Maynard Smith, a dirt-poor farm boy from the Pantego Swamp area of Beaufort County, wondered, "What kind of fool contraption has that young'un made now?"

So recalled the Rev. R. M. Gradeless, a man who knew Smith. "Some people thought it was a blasphemous thing," he said.

For in 1889, 14 years before the Wright Brothers would make history with their flying contraption at Kill Devil Hill, John Maynard Smith built an airplane.

That teen-ager John Smith built a flying machine is a documented fact. Gradeless remembers hearing his father tell of going to watch it fly. Grover Cleveland, president of the United States, saw the airplane.

What makes the feat even more remarkable is that the young John Smith, whose education went no further than what he could learn from a spelling book, invented his airplane without having any access to the research of the aviation pioneers. He read no books or learned papers, he attended no scientific conferences, he had no university research departments helping him. He did it by himself, alone on his farm, thinking all along that he was the first.

He never even saw a picture of an airplane until he held his own plane in his hands.

"I got to know him pretty well," Gradeless said. "We'd walk home after church, and I became close to him. Like all young boys, I asked him questions all the time. He didn't like to talk about his invention, a lot of people still made fun of him, but if he thought you were sincere he'd tell you about it.

"He told me he got the idea from looking at big birds, like hawks. He looked at their wings and tried to build wings like theirs, curved."

But fame was to elude John Smith all his life. Folks in the neighborhood, where Smith lived with his widowed father on their five-acre farm supplemented by part-time work as a mill hand, used to come on Sundays to watch the marvelous toy.

In 1893, former neighbor George Gaskins first saw the airplane. Gaskins was an official with the Philadelphia Navy Yard and immediately saw the potential the "toy" had for the future.

Gaskins took the airplane to Washington and presented it to President Cleveland in the summer of 1893.

The president was not impressed. He told Gaskins that if the young Beaufort County farmboy would build a plane that would haul a man, the government would be interested.

Cleveland, in fact, is quoted as having said after the

meeting: "There is one fool in North Carolina, I know, who wants to put a propeller on the front of a ship, and any fool knows that if you put a propeller on the front of a ship, it would push the ship backwards."

Gaskins came home with the sad report. It would take $400 to build a full-scale airplane, he and Smith figured, and no one had enough faith in the young man to risk their money.

"Mr. Smith said he was so disgusted and frustrated that he put the airplane in the barn and only took it out a few times," Gradeless said.

"There used to be a lot of drummers (traveling salesmen) coming through here and they'd hear of the airplane and want to see it. Finally, after showing it to so many people, it was stolen and never heard from again."

"And John Smith never built another one."

Smith lived out his life in the Belhaven area, working at a barrel factory for most of his life. He died Jan. 12, 1963, an anonymous man.

Oops

Wilson.

Drum roll, please.

"Ladies and gentlemen, please direct your attention to the small platform 110 feet in the air where the amazing, stupefying, and fearless Professor Danton is preparing for his leap.

"And now he leans forward and ... THERE HE GOES!"

Oops!

Professor Danton missed by just a tad when he made his last jump in Goldsboro that warm night of May 13, 1904, and as he lay dying next door to the Wayne County Courthouse, he was heard to say, "I must go back to Wilson to be buried with my friends."

Danton's stone marker lies just to the right as you enter the impressive main gate of Maplewood Cemetery here in Wilson. It bears the epitaph, "Leaped from life into eternity, May 13, 1904."

Professor Danton also leaped straight into the hallowed

halls of Rogers' Gallery of Unusual People, Places and Things.

His name was Antoine Szegadi Danton, a native of Budapest, Hungary and during his time was the world's "most intrepid high diver."

He came to Wilson during May 1904 with the Johnny J. Jones Carnival. He was a tremendous hit, doing his high-diving act from 90 feet up in the air. Folks came from all over to see The Professor, as he was known, and he spent most of his ground-level hours stealing the hearts of a number of local ladies.

But one, a lovely lady from a good family, stole his in return. Wilson girls do things like that.

The star-crossed lovers decided early it was not to be, him being a traveling man and all, so The Professor packed up at the end of the week and went on down the road to Goldsboro.

But he had been such a hit in Wilson that a five-car train jammed with 500 people went from Wilson to Goldsboro to see him do his thing one more time.

The Professor's tent was a popular place that night with Wilsonians by the score going in and out to visit. Rumor has it that a goodly amount of Wayne's finest stumphole whiskey was put away that spring night as the country people came to call on the Hungarian.

I'm not one to speak unkindly of the departed, so let's just say that when the Professor walked out of his tent a few minutes after 11 p.m. he was seen to stagger. Some said he was feeling poorly. Some said he was blind drunk.

He climbed to 110 feet that last time, carrying out his promise that he was going to be the highest diver of them all.

From all accounts, he certainly was. In more ways than one.

The idea was that his trusted assistant down below would set fire to the oil on the tank of water and then the Professor would set fire to his oil-drenched costume and plunge ablazing through the night sky.

The assistant lit the tank and the Professor lit his costume.

But then the fire in the tank went out, so the Professor stood there, burning, while it was relighted. Finally he jumped to the collected AAAAAHHHHHS of the crowd.

He missed.

He was given a musical sendoff by the circus band which gathered and played, "Hello Central, Give Me Heaven" as his body was removed from the circus lot.

He lies in Wilson today, where he asked to be buried, and for many years his grave was almost a shrine for visiting circus troupes. They would come to pay their respects and leave a wreath, but as the years went on, the memory of the fearless high diver who fell in love and to his death within the same week faded.

No Dirt, No Holes

There are times, not many mind you, when I do indeed miss "the good old days."

I miss them for about eight seconds until I remember how it used to be, back before machines took over the harvesting of tobacco.

We rose before dawn — it was cooler then, and damp. Bare feet left dry tracks in the moist dirt as we headed for the barn. My job was to hook up the mules to the drags, while the grown folks emptied a barn of just-cured tobacco.

It was a miserable way to start a day.

Cured tobacco was dirty. Fine sand stuck to each leaf, sending down a grimy shower every time a stick — on which the leaves were draped for drying — was touched. By dawn all of us were sweaty and dirty and the day's work had not even begun.

There are few sights more imposing than a tobacco field at dawn. A cluster of men and boys stand at one end of the first row, looking out at that green expanse, knowing that by day's end we would walk up and down every row, stalk by stalk.

The croppers were the kings of my world, my youthful idols. They did the hardest, most tormenting work man has ever devised.

The croppers, four abreast, walked between the head-high stalks, bent from the waist, reaching down into that humid darkness, unpenetrated for weeks by the sun's rays.

They would pull off the bottom two or three leaves, leaving this leaf, taking that one, looking for the ones with the slight yellow tinge. They did it as much by feel as anything else.

They pulled two leaves from the stalk on their right, turned, pulled two leaves from the stalk on their left, like robots, not thinking, not feeling, just doing. It was the only way to survive that painful monotony.

The freshly pulled leaves were tucked under their left arms, packed tightly until they could carry no more. My job was to be there when they called, to take the load and pile it in a 4-foot by 8-foot sled called a drag. Four croppers, working eight rows, could keep a kid busy and it was always the kids who were draggers.

The sweating, cursing, muscled men bent over hour after sun-baked hour, dodging snakes, ignoring flies, grabbing those leaves, down deep between the stalks, where the breeze never blew.

It was called "getting the monkey on your back," that time when too much heat caught up to you and you passed out, or went crazy, or cried or got sick to your stomach. I've seen grown men do all four.

Once my drag was full, I would slap the limp cotton reins on the mule's back and we'd head for the barn. May the Lord have mercy on you if you dared to ride. Mules worked. Boys walked.

It was not easy. Top-heavy drags turned over easily and no shame compared to having to reload a toppled drag. Besides, it got the tobacco dirty and the barn hands hated you for it.

Farm kids these days may find it hard to believe, but 20 years ago we cared about the leaf. We prized full leaves, no dirt, no holes. Now it is handled with pitchforks.

The barn was a woman's domain, women with arms and legs as strong as any men. They stood 10 to 12 hours a day, gracefully stringing tobacco on sticks. They took pride in their work, not only in the speed, but in their touch. Shake a stick of their tobacco and not one leaf fell out.

On either side of the stringers stood the handers, the bottom level of that bygone social order. They were usually girls and their job was to grab two to three leaves and hand them to the stringer who artfully looped on the left and then on the right, an unbroken ballet in the sultry heat.

At day's end, after the croppers had walked miles and sweated gallons, they came back to the barn to hang the sticky tobacco so it could be cured.

Usually it was dark when we finished, just time enough for a quiet meal, a quick bath and sleep.

Another field was waiting for another dawn.

A Soldier's Odyssey

South Mills.

The Confederate soldiers defending this northeastern North Carolina town on April 19, 1862, first saw the woman during the heat of the battle that raged over these swampy fields.

They were dug into the south of the town, facing 5,000 Yankee troops. Between the lines, in an open field, was an old house.

Suddenly the Rebel boys saw the figure of a young woman break from the Union lines. Carrying a baby in her arms, she ran as hard as she could for the safety of the old house in the middle of the battlefield.

Henry Dixon, the aristocratic son of wealthy South Carolina planters, saw the woman and baby reach the house safely. He could also see that the house was being ripped to shreds by the cannon balls and rifle fire.

So the young man — who had left his home in the blood-pounding days when the war was young and every Southerner thought it would be over in a month — dropped his gun and dashed across the open battlefield for the little house.

He was too late. A cannon blast had killed the woman, striking her in the face. But the baby she was carrying was alive, smeared in its mother's blood, trying to wake her up as it sat by her unrecognizable body.

Dixon grabbed the infant and ran back to his lines, somehow making it through the fire to safety. Maybe Providence was on his side. Maybe the enemy soldiers couldn't bring themselves to shoot at Dixon and the baby.

Dixon gave the child to Dr. R. A. Lewis, the unit surgeon, and went back to being a soldier. Lewis eventually took the child, a baby girl, to his home in Richmond where she would live.

But Lewis did something else that fateful day. When the battle was over, he went out looking for survivors and to oversee burial of the dead. He found the woman's body in the house and removed a locket from her breast, slipping it into his pocket and planning one day to give it to the little girl.

Henry Dixon survived the war and returned to South Carolina. But Sherman's army had gotten there first, and the only thing left was blackened rubble and the graves of his parents.

Among the missing was his wife, the former Mary Singleton. No one could tell him what had happened to Mary. All the neighbors knew was that she had left South Carolina during the war, taking their only child with her. Some said she went to Norfolk, looking for Henry.

Dixon went in search of Mary and the baby. He followed her trail to Norfolk, but there it died.

His search and his money ended, Dixon returned to South Carolina and began the long work of rebuilding his plantation and his life. But then there was a windfall of money and the search was on again.

Back to Norfolk he went, this time for a month, but with the same dead-end result. Mary Singleton Dixon had vanished.

Brokenhearted, Dixon decided to drop in on his old friend Lewis before returning home. On his way to Lewis' Richmond home, Dixon happened by a school while recess was on.

There, in that place of childish laughter, was a little girl playing in the schoolyard.

Dixon asked the little girl her name. She said it was May Darling. He asked her where she lived. She said with Dr. Lewis.

Dixon went to the Lewis home. Lewis told him that May

Darling wasn't really her name. It was the little girl Dixon had saved from the battlefield, and since they didn't know her last name, they had taken to calling her May Darling.

Lewis showed Dixon something else that day, the locket he had taken from the dead woman' breast.

Dixon, with shaking fingers, opened the locket.

On one side was a picture of the little girl.

On the other side was a picture of Henry Dixon.

The dead woman with the locket had been Mary Singleton Dixon, Henry's wife. She had gone looking for her husband, and he had found her that bloody day, too late only by the seconds it takes a cannon ball to fly.

The child that Henry Dixon had saved so long ago was his daughter.

One Brief Shining Moment

November 22, 1978.

Camelot shone so brilliantly just 15 years ago.

He was young and vital, what all of us so desperately needed after the doldrums of the 1950s and the beloved Uncle Ike.

Jack and Jackie, friendly names for friendly people. We loved them and they loved us back. They had funny Boston accents and mop-headed kids. They were everything we wanted to be.

And then, 15 years ago today, a miserable misfit with a cheap rifle gunned him down and the dream turned sour.

I think of John F. Kennedy from time to time and, like everyone else, my memories are both crystal clear and mercifully hazy. I know he was in political trouble, his popularity sagging in the polls, his legislative programs mired in Congress. I know he had the CIA plan and execute an invasion of a neighboring nation, but also I remember, how well I remember, the long days and nights when he went one-on-one with Khrushchev during the Cuban missile crisis.

At the time of the nuclear showdown, I was a technician with a Nike Hercules missile outfit, stationed in the West Texas desert. We held fast during those days, but friends were sent to Florida to man their missiles with the nuclear warheads, facing the Cubans just 90 miles or so away.

For many people, it was an exercise in spine-tingling diplomacy. For soldiers, it was the real thing. I still remember the time we scrambled because a Mexican airliner failed to instantly identify itself. The people on that airliner never knew how close they came to becoming a fireball. We were hair-trigger ready, scared to death on the one hand and eager to see those birds fly on the other.

But through it all there was John Kennedy, unflappable in public, who knows how in private. We knew that whatever he told us to do it would be the right thing, Camelot had that kind of magic for us.

I was still in Texas when Camelot died, still in the desert, still playing with missiles. It was lunch time, a friendly game of pool in the dayroom after lunch. A TV set blared down the hall.

Someone came in the dayroom and said quietly, "Hey, there's something on the news about Kennedy."

The name still held magic for the missilemen. After all, hadn't he told us in a private message during the tense hours of the missile crisis that we were the front line of defense, that no matter what happened, we must not fail. Our birds must fly if he asked them to. And they would have flown, Mr. President, you can bet on it.

We crowded in the TV room. As long as I live, I'll never forget the sight of Walter Cronkite in shirt sleeves, with his voice choking, telling us that the man we revered was probably dead.

It was two blocks from the dayroom to our duty station. As the Texas sun shone down — it was a beautiful day in the desert — hurt, angry, confused missilemen headed back to their jobs. No one ran. There didn't seem to be a reason to, they just walked slowly across an open, sandy field.

We were usually a happy group, laughing and joking while working. Morale was high, we had been told we were the cream of the crop, America's elite in the still-growing space age.

But now the man who told us that was dead. The man who counted on us to save the nation was gone, wiped out by a creep with a lousy rifle.

I'll never forget the scene that day as the missilemen went back to work. They stretched across that dusty field, each man walking alone, head down, lost in his private grief. No one spoke, no one waved, no one said a word.

There didn't seem to be anything to say.

There didn't seem to be anything to believe in anymore.

Poor Whistler's Mama

Clarkton.

I have learned a Great Truth and one of the best-kept secrets in modern America that I will now share with you:

Did you ever wonder where they got all those complicated plots for soap operas?

They all came from North Carolina, specifically from the life of a woman who used to live in this town. She didn't write them, but she sure lived them.

Her name was Anna Mathilda McNeill, known around the world because her son painted her picture — a picture that has gone down in history as "Whistler's Mother."

Anna was born in Clarkton in 1804 at a plantation called Oak Forest. The plantation was destroyed in a fire.

She had a brother named William who was a cadet at West Point and one summer he brought a classmate home for vacation, a lad named George Washington Whistler, nicknamed "Pipes" for no reason that I know.

Well, Anna fell for Pipes in a big way and when her family moved to New York so Daddy McNeill could do medical research, she was delighted.

Anna's best friend in New York was a girl named Mary Swift, daughter of the medical officer at West Point, and the two girls had a fine time double-dating with the boys, Pipes and William.

But when the boys graduated, Pipes up and marries Mary, since her father was a high-ranking officer and the young lieutenant was no dummy. Anna sat home, reportedly not too bitter; but I don't believe that.

What should happen but Mary dies, leaving Pipes with three kids and faithful Anna waiting in the wings. She was 27 by this time, and lovely, so she made her move and married the young widower.

That should have been the end of the saga, but bad times were just beginning for the future Whistler's mother.

The couple had a son, James Abbott McNeill Whistler, but shortly thereafter, Joseph, son of Mary, dies and another son, Charles is born.

Pipes goes off to Russia to build a railroad for the Czar, but while he's on the boat, their son Kirk dies. Anna then leaves to join Pipes, but son Charles kicks off in mid-Atlantic.

After they get to Russia Baby John is born. Daughter Deborah goes to England to visit and when Pipes goes to bring her home, guess what? Baby John dies.

Then Pipes dies at age 45 or so, leaving Anna in Russia with I'm not sure how many kids since I lost count about then.

Anyway, the family, or what's left of it, goes back to the U. S. of A. and James enrolls in West Point, flunks out, gets a job in Washington, gets fired and ends up living in sin in Paris with a redhead.

Anna comes back to North Carolina, but she boards a clipper ship in Fayetteville, runs the blockade under Yankee cannon balls and ends up in Paris, where James won't speak to her for two years because she raises cain about his girl friend.

Anna's sight is going fast, so aged and blind and all alone in Paris and with kids buried all over the world and a son living with a degenerate redhead, she has nothing to do but sit in her room by the fire and think about all this.

One day, while sitting there and wondering what the heck she did to deserve it, Son James the painter comes in, sees her sitting there and paints her picture.

But did he have the decency to call it "Whistler's Mother"? Not on your tintype. He called it "Arrangements in Grey and Black." It didn't get to be known as Whistler's Mother until well after her death.

Soap operas pale by comparison.

A Time by the Sea

Carolina Beach.

Not all love stories are about people. Some are about places:

It was different then, back on those moonlit nights when he was young and she was pretty.

He fell in love with her the first day they met. It was a Saturday. The sun had shown through the back window of the '55 Chevy all the way from his farm home to where she waited for him by the sea, making him anxious to see her.

They'd met once before, but not like this. Not with time to fall in love. The first time had been brief, too brief, but now there were eight glorious days.

She was there when the car stopped, resting by the sea in the Carolina sun. He didn't notice how her pavement burned his farm-toughened feet. He didn't notice how his father smiled as he told him to be careful and have fun with her that week.

He wooed her by morning's chilly light and afternoon's blazing heat that summer by the sea and she returned his love, teaching him in her own gentle way how to be a man. She taught him to swagger and gave him reason to. She let him meet girls. She let him savor the forbidden taste of beer. She let him stay up late, sitting with her and looking out to Africa, wondering what was there and if he'd ever get his chance to see.

She was patient with him and he learned and loved her for it.

And then the eight days were gone and he said goodby on a Sunday morning when there was no one around to hear.

He saw her again during the years that followed, after he'd had a chance to see across the ocean and after he'd found himself a wife and after he thought he'd forgotten her.

He took his wife and children to see her once or twice and she was kind, but it wasn't the same. She was older and more tattered. She'd shared her favors with too many young men. She'd taught them as she had him and it showed. She was more frayed around the edges and it took a special kind of moonlight to make her look young again.

But he went back again last week, alone this time, and they met again by the sea. For an hour he was 14 and she was lovely. He walked her boardwalk and passed her boarded-up bingo stands and gift shops.

He stopped for coffee where once he ate foot-long hot dogs at midnight. He stood for a moment where the fishing pier used to be and where now there is nothing but black pilings holding up fat sea gulls.

Carolina Beach didn't look so young and pretty anymore. The sea and the children and the strolling grandparents and the young farm families and the soldiers and, most of all, the young boys like himself had had their way with her once too often and she was tired.

But that didn't matter that sunny afternoon by the sea. They were together again and he loved her as much as ever.

"Take care of yourself," he said to her as he left.

"Take care of her," he said, to anyone who would listen.

Rumors, Gossip
And Baldfaced Lies

Here's a secret. Columnists are terrible persons when it comes to stealing funny stories from each other. If one of us comes up with a good one, it is a safe bet that the rest of us will read it and find a way to rip it off and pass it on to our readers. We do it for two reasons:

We all love good stories.

And we are all as lazy as snakes in August.

This tale comes my way from Bob Terrell in Asheville, who stole it from Dick Bothwell in St. Petersburg, who ripped it off from somebody in St. Paul, Minn., who got it from who knows where.

Seems a young couple was having a spat one morning. Words flew hot and heavy, and then a silence so thick you could cut it settled on the love nest.

They stormed around the house, ignoring each other, slamming doors, banging pots and huffing until the lady had a problem with the long zipper in the back of her dress.

She backed up to her fuming hubby and silently pointed over her shoulder to the zipper, indicating that if he was any kind of husband at all he would zip it up for her.

He grabbed the zipper tab and, with a quick slide, pulled it to the top. Then — as they used to say — the devil flew in him and he couldn't resist. Up and down the zipper went, zip-zip-zip, as the hubby let all of his anger out.

Then the zipper broke, leaving the lady standing in her favorite dress with a broken zipper, mad as a wet hen at her husband and late for work. The final straw came when hubby had to cut her out of the now-worthless dress.

She thought about it all day, plotting revenge against the creep she loved. The more she thought the madder she got.

Her chance for revenge came that night as she came home from work. There, sticking out from under the family car, was a pair of legs wearing pants. Grunts and sounds of heavy mechanical work came from the greasy darkness underneath.

The lady tried, but she couldn't resist. This was her chance.

She leaned over, grasped the pants zipper in her hand and zipped up and down like crazy, a blur of motion, until her anger abated.

Feeling smug, she walked in the house and headed for the kitchen.

There, sitting at the kitchen table, was her husband.

She stammered for a moment, felt faint and sat down. She sat quietly for a moment and then, in a tiny voice and not really wanting to hear the answer, asked, "Who is that under the car?"

"That's Bill. He came to help me fix the muffler," her husband replied. Then she told him what had happened.

He, at least, thought it was funny, and the couple decided the only decent thing to do would be to explain to Bill why a neighbor lady was playing with his fly. They went back outside to where Bill's legs still protruded from under the car.

"Bill?" called the husband.

Silence.

"Bill?" called the lady, nervously this time.

Still nothing.

The couple grabbed Bill's legs and pulled him out.

Bill was lying there, knocked cold as a cucumber with a nasty gash on his forehead from banging his head when a strange hand had fumbled with his fly.

Bill recovered nicely. He thought it was funny, once the swelling went down.

Amana on the Run

Pinetops.

"The only thing I've sold today is heat lamps, propane torches and pipe insulation," Steve Burress blustered when I walked in. "Man there ain't no water running no where around here."

Which is understandable, considering it had been a whopping 4 degrees the night before and the winter sun had pushed it up only to 17 degrees by afternoon. Pinetops and my feet were frozen solid.

It being that cold, the only logical thing for Burress to talk about was refrigerators.

"I'd always wanted me one of them refrigerators with the water in the door," he said, while I nestled stove-side with a cup of his coffee.

"We're having trouble with the one we had at home, so when Mama and Daddy went on vacation, I decided to buy them one.

"On the way back, out there on that four-lane stretch, I got to looking at the big box out the back window of the pickup when that Amana name on the box commenced to getting smaller and smaller. It got smaller and further away until it fell off right out there on the highway, with what must have been 400 cars coming up behind it.

"I figured that was the worst thing that could happen, so some folks helped me get it loaded back on the truck and I came on to Pinetops.

"It wasn't hurt or nothing, just a couple of dents, so I got two boys to help me with it. They were up on the porch going into the house when it and the two of them slap disappeared.

"The durn porch had caved in.

"Then we took three doors off the hinges, but it still wouldn't go through the den door. We took it the other way around, taking off two more doors, and it still wouldn't fit.

"We finally picked it up and got it in there someway, and then we hooked up the plumbing and danged if it didn't leak.

"Then we tried to slide it into place where the old one

had been and the place was too small. We ended up having to cut down the cabinet.

"I swear to you, I've never had so much trouble trying to be nice to somebody in my life."

About that time one-third of the Pinetops police department came in in the person of David Harrell.

"I need a bottle of that propane for a torch," he said. "Every water pipe at my house is frozen up.

"If you hear three rapid-fire shots, that means I've set the house on fire so y'all come with the fire truck."

"You ain't the only one whose got trouble with pipes," someone else said. "There's this one old boy in town who's been trying everything he could think of for three days to thaw his pipes.

"He finally found out his son had turned the water off."

Please Execute Johnny

Roanoke Rapids.

William Branch, principal of the high school here, says he doesn't think it came from Roanoke Rapids.

Mrs. Lucille Dickens, secretary in the school system office, says she's heard about things like it, but she doesn't think it came from Roanoke Rapids either.

But whoever sent it to me in the mail said it did.

All it is is a newspaper. The letter with it was unsigned. I couldn't read the postmark and I can't tell what paper the clipping came from.

"These are excuses parents have sent to school for their kids," the letter said. "They were collected by a secretary in the Roanoke Rapids schools and sent to me. I thought they were funny and thought you might like to read them."

I loved them and thought you would too. I did change a name here or there, but other than that this is the way they came, spelling, grammar and all.

"Dear School: Please axiuse Johnny for being absent on January 28, 29, 30, 31, 32."

"Johnny had an acre on his side."

"Mary could not come to school because she was bothered by very close veins."

"Johnny has been absent because he had had two teeth taken out of his face."

"My son is under the doctor's care and should not take P.E. Please execute him."

"Please excuse Mary from P.E. for a few days. Yesterday she fell out of a tree and misplaced her hip."

"Please excuse Johnny Friday. He had loose vowels."

"Johnny was absent yesterday because he was playing football. He was hurt in the growing part."

"Please excuse Johnny for being. It was his father's fault."

"Mary was absent December 15-16 because she had a fever, sore throat, headache and upset stomach. Her sister was also sick, fever and sore throat. Her brother had a low grade fever and ached all over. I wasn't the best either, sore throat and fever. There must be flu going around ..."

Now I'm scared to write a note for my pair. Since most excuse notes are hastily scrawled while trying to keep the eggs from burning, the dog from eating your shoes and the eyes open, there is no telling what all of us have written at one time or another.

The Truth or Close to It

Four Oaks.

Rayphard Lee sat in his small bedroom in the 110-year-old Johnston County house in which he lives the other day and told me stories:

"You probably won't believe none of this, but my daddy told me it was true.

"Back in them days, folks used to have a good way of quail huntin'.

"My grandaddy Edward got to where he would sit on a creekbank what had a log lyin' cross it and he'd whistle up quails.

"Folks used to be better whistlers than they are now, don't you know, and pretty soon them quails would come a walkin' up lined up in a straight line, about 12 of 'em at the time.

"My grandaddy Edward would sight his rifle along that

log and when he'd fire his gun he'd blow the heads off ever one of them quails and they'd fall in the creek, all with one shot.

"Then my grandaddy Edward would go down to the creek and catch 'em as they floated by.

"Speakin' a creeks, one time my Uncle Raney got up at first light to go catch him some red fins down to Hockaday Bridge. He was under the bridge when he heard somebody.

"He went up there and it was my Uncle Tim. He told Uncle Raney he'd walked over to Smithfield to pick up a singletree and he saw where they was sellin' flour 10 cents cheaper by the sack so he bought him a hundred pounds of it to bring home and he'd just stopped to rest just that one time.

"I reckon he did have to stop to rest, 'cause it was near 10 miles from there to Smithfield and a hundred pounds is a load.

"And one time they were a killing hogs. Did you know that back then they had to call 'em hogs up and shoot them like wild game? Well anyway, one morning before day Uncle Tim was sent to get the salt they needed, so he just stepped up to Selma and walked back with 300 pounds a salt on his shoulder and that's near seven mile.

"This place you're sitting used to be my mama's house and one night when my daddy was courtin' her he came walkin' up here four or five mile and met up with some of his old friends who had 'em some of that apple brandy and they got pretty much drunk.

"Now Uncle Raney — I told you 'bout him, didn't I? — lived down the road and he had him some hogs that used to feed right by where my daddy had to walk home. Daddy was walkin' home that night after all that brandy and courtin' and he come up on them hogs in the dark of the night. Daddy heard 'em, especially that old sow a-poppin' her lips and he knowed he couldn't go walkin' right by her in the dark. Some of them old sows is mean, don't you know?

"He had him a fiddle under his arm so he put it under his chin and went to drawin' down on that old E-string.

"That old sow went to squealin' and squallin' and busted out of there. She hit that creek and Daddy could hear her belly slappin' the water like boat paddles.

"Daddy scared them hogs to death that night and they wouldn't come back for a week.

"Of course, I don't know that all this is true, don't you know, but it's what my daddy used to tell me."

Class A Hissie

Funny stories are the peanuts of literature. Sample one and you're hooked.

Dow Pender of Raleigh called to share this one.

The lady of the house, worried that a recent cold snap might harm her plants out on the front porch, decided she'd bring them in for the night.

She lugged them into the house and, as she set the last plant down, a small green snake, which had been enjoying the weak sun while stretched out on a small branch, slithered onto the floor.

The woman, who like a lot of us sensible people think snakes are creatures of evil to be avoided at all cost, came completely unglued.

She began screaming at the top of her lungs, jumping up and down in the middle of the cluttered floor and having what can only be called a Class A Hissie.

The husband, who was wearing nothing but a smile while taking a hot shower, heard the commotion over the running water.

Thinking his wife must be in dire peril, the husband, sans smile, came charging down the stairs like a drippy White Knight of yore.

The snake, which was barely awake but getting a trifle nervous, was now faced with a screaming banshee on one side and a wet, naked man lunging at him from the other. The creature headed underneath the sofa.

That didn't help. Pointing under the sofa, the woman kept up her fit. The husband, turning a lovely shade of goosebump purple, decided the only way he'd ever finish his shower in time to avoid a serious case of all-over frostbite was to remove the snake — a job he didn't relish but one he felt duty-bound to perform.

Hubby, no fan of snakes, then nervously knelt down to peer under the dark sofa in search of the panicky snake.

Enter Bowzer, the family dog.

Bowzer, drawn by the ruckus, ambled in to check out this latest horror to befall his masters. The dog took one look at the woman and knew intelligent communication with her was impossible.

He spotted the no-longer dripping, but still naked as a jaybird, husband kneeling by the sofa. Not having seen his master in such a pose before, the dog was baffled. But being a good dog, he decided the only thing to do was to find out who this was and why the lady of the house was screaming at his backside.

So the dog crept up quietly behind the muttering and shivering husband, whose fingers were within an inch of the snake. The dog applied his very cold nose to the portion of the man's anatomy that was most exposed to the elements.

Already as tense as a new screen-door spring, the touch of the cold dog's nose in a most vulnerable spot was all it took. The husband yelled, jumped up and fainted dead away.

Now the woman, faced with a man-eating snake under her sofa, a naked and wet husband passed out on the floor and a dog running crazily around the room, was at the end of her rope. She did the only thing left — called for help.

The rescue squad arrived moments later. They roared up, dashed into the house like television heroes and proceeded to efficiently scoop up the passed-out Papa.

The two burly heroes got the husband on the stretcher in record time and were just fixing to go out the door on their mercy mission.

Meanwhile, the snake figured it was now or never and made a frantic squirm for the now-open front door, arriving at the same moment as our heroes.

Both stretcher bearers saw the snake at the same time and their nerve left them like water from a busted hose.

They screamed and threw up their hands in fright.

Since stretchers will not float in midair, the stretcher and the naked hubby crashed to the floor, dumping hubby onto the wet carpet and sending the lady into a new fit of screaming.

And, to add insult to injury, hubby suffered a broken arm.

I would have paid good money to be there when this spaced-out bunch finally arrived at the hospital emergency room and tried to explain it all to the steely-eyed nurse at the front desk.

And Bowzer has completed his 3,574th revolution of the living room and is still running.

Folks Not Easily Forgotten

Fayetteville.

This would be the last time.

The girl was leaving home and this was the place where the family would begin to come apart.

They sat in the last four seats on the outside row of the Trailways bus station, facing away from the crowd, seeking privacy in a public place.

The girl wore a white sundress and held a bright red carnation in her lap. A white paper bag lay between her ankles, a bag of magazines and candy bars for the long bus ride to Washington, D. C.

Washington.

The marble dream that has lured Carolina farm girls for generations.

Washington.

No more tobacco fields or pimply boys in pickup trucks. No more bare feet and corn cribs. She was grown now and Washington was waiting.

Mama sat to her right, dirty feet stuck in run-down sandals. Mama leaned over and said something private to the girl.

The girl looked back at her mama, perhaps for the last time as a little girl, and said softly, "I will Mama, I will. Don't worry."

A tear slid softly down the girl's cheek.

Daddy sat to her left. He stared at the wall in front of him, not moving or blinking. It was ending all too soon.

A brother sat on the end, beside the father. At first he tried to talk, but he got no answers and fell silent, mesmerized by the drama he didn't understand.

The end was coming. He didn't know how it would be different without the girl at home, but he knew it would be.

What little talking there had been was ending.

Each lost in thought, they tried to get through a time they had known would come someday. And now it was here. It had come so quickly.

The girl chewed her fingernails and toyed with the flower.

Mama stared at her left sandal.

Daddy shifted his gaze to the floor.

Brother watched a janitor work.

Suddenly, as if no one had really expected it to happen, a bus grunted and wheezed into the parking lot. The family knew somehow that the bus named "Express" was the one even before the announcer started talking.

The boy led the way to the door. Mama and Daddy walked on either side of the girl as they went outside into the hazy, gassy heat.

She hugged her brother first and then her Mama.

Finally she turned to her Daddy and gave him a hug he would remember so long as he lived.

Then she was gone. She disappeared into the bus named "Express," swallowed up by the big seats and the tinted windows.

Daddy walked away first. He had seen and felt enough. The pain of this hot day would be slow to fade. He walked by the seats where the family sat that last time.

There, forgotten, was the red carnation, gleaming in stark relief against the black plastic seat.

He picked it up, looked at the bus for a moment and then turned away, walking slowly up the hallway.

Mama caught him about halfway to the door. She

walked beside him, holding his other hand, and quietly, they were gone.

They had brought a little girl to a bus station.

They had watched a woman leave.

Heads and Tails

Rocky Mount.

Six days a week, at exactly 9 a.m., a group of this city's most prestigious citizens descend a dark, trashy-looking stairwell.

They enter a cluttered basement room under an old building, a room with a giant pinup on one wall and a sign that reads, "Those of you who think you know everything are very annoying to us who do."

For the next 30 minutes, that select group of Rocky Mount's best, drink a dark, savory liquid made from foreign-grown plants and say some of the most insulting things you can imagine about each other.

They gamble every day — and frequently cheat — and slander hallowed state institutions, saying terrible things like, "We're not partial, we don't care who beats Carolina."

But before you call the law, let me introduce you to the Howard Street Heads and Tails Society, a 40-year-old tradition of coffee drinking, good times and practical jokes.

Formed about 1938, the society has met every day, except Sundays, Christmas and New Year's Day, ever since.

"Most of these people are too sorry to work, so they drink coffee," one of them told me in a secret tongue-in-cheek aside. After being privileged to join them one morning not long ago, all I can say is, Lord, ain't it the truth.

Pardon me if I don't get all the names in but you're lucky to escape with wallet intact when flipping coins with characters like Bugs Barringer, writer and photographer; Vernon Sechriest, editor emeritus of the Rocky Mount Telegram; Al Rabil, a retired construction company owner and chief joke teller; Don Cole, a druggist and absolutely the worst gambler in the world; Mae Bell Woods, director of the Children's Museum, caretaker of Percy, my favorite owl, cookie-maker extraordinaire and the group's only woman; Christian White, a Methodist minister who claims he was born on Christmas Day, and Tom Hicks, the only Carolina fan in the bunch and a man of infinite patience and good taste.

I haven't the foggiest notion of how this got started. I asked a lot of people, and they all tried to tell me, but when this crowd meets for coffee and flipping quarters to see who pays, don't expect a lot of serious conversation. If they told me, I forgot the details.

But apparently, they got to meeting in Worth Joyner's hardware store about 1938 where they'd match for soft drinks. Nobody said, but Worth probably evicted them, and they went through several lunch counters and restaurants before being thrown out for general rowdiness. Then they discovered the basement of the old People's Bank building, and there they stay.

Sechriest is the rules chairman, Barringer said, "But it really doesn't matter because he changes the rules all the time. Besides, what can you expect from a man who has the worst garden in Rocky Mount, not half as good as mine?"

To decide who pays, the members flip coins. They cheat outrageously, and cleverly, and it is amazing I made it out with car payment intact. I'm sure it was because they wanted me to write good things about them. Next time I'll lose.

They do terrible things to each other, like the time Bugs planted rye grass in Sechriest's lawn spelling out "UNC." Vernon, you must understand, is the biggest Duke fan this side of Terry Sanford. Then there was the time Bugs and Don put a skimpily-clad mannequin on Vernon's lawn.

Then they gave the preacher a joke gift of cigarettes, dice and booze for Christmas.

These people are friends, in the old way when friendship meant something special, when a friend wasn't afraid to do anything for another friend.

Or to a friend, now that I think of it.

Mattie Dixon, Citizen

Grifton.

Her name is Mrs. Mattie Dixon.

She is 73 years old, a great-grandmother and the Grifton Chamber of Commerce's Outstanding Citizen of the Year.

She is also black.

"It made me feel happy and rejoiceful to accomplish something like that," she told me the other day as we enjoyed a spring afternoon.

"I called my sister in Brooklyn, N. Y., and she said, 'In Grifton? You must have moved. I never thought Grifton would get to that.'

"Well, to tell you the truth I didn't either. When I was growing up here I never thought I'd live to see the day when a colored woman would be chosen like that by white folks.

"I was born right across Contentnea Creek over there. I can remember the whistles blowing up and down the river at night and all of us children running out to see the boats. On Sunday evenings in the summer we'd all walk up to the depot to see who was getting off the train and who was getting on.

"My daddy always made me go to school and I had a teacher at Grifton School who was the most beautiful, precious and nicest person I've ever known. She made a real impression on me and I decided if she could teach, so could I. When she found out what I wanted to be she'd come to my house on Sunday and help me with my books.

"I finished the eighth grade here and then worked my way through Kinston College to finish 12 grades. I still wanted to be a teacher so I read all the books I could find. My pastor even used to loan me books.

"I took my certification test in Kinston and they told me they'd mail me the results. I went to that mailbox every day looking to hear from Raleigh. When the letter came I hugged it to my heart and ran all the way back to the house before I opened it. I didn't need to open it because I just knew I had passed.

"And when I opened it and saw I'd made it I had me a hallelujah time. I've never been so happy in my life."

That was in 1928. She taught school until 1942 when her husband was taken sick. She quit to take care of him for 12 long years, giving him all her attention.

"He was my husband," she said simply. "He came first. After he died I buried myself in church activities and taking care of people."

The slight little woman, hurrying from one humble house to another in the part of town they still call "colored town" became a familiar sight in Grifton.

"Folks used to ask me what I'd do if I come up on one of them drunkards in the dark. It wouldn't bother me a bit. They all call me Ma and they respect me and love me, because I treat them right.

"My Bible — and I keep it by my bed — says God is no respecter of persons and I'm not either. I don't care if they are drunkards or black or white, I'll help them if I can.

"I started working in white people's houses after my husband died, and do you know those children I helped raise still come to see me and write me letters? When they have babies I know about it as soon as their parents do. I know where everyone of them is and what they're doing. They come to see me as soon as they see their own family."

When racial trouble came to Pitt County, it was only natural that Mrs. Dixon would find herself in the middle of it.

"A bunch of those outsiders came in and said the colored children weren't supposed to go to school as a protest. I told them right off that my grandson Johnny Mack Willis was going to go to school and that the rest of them should because we need their education.

"I had prayed to God to let me live long enough to see that boy I raised graduate from school. One time they said they would whip him if he went to school. Two of them came in a car here and stopped the school bus in the road.

"I put my gun under my apron and stood out there in the yard and told them that the first one to get out of that car to whip Johnny Mack Willis had to whip me first. I aimed to keep that pistol going until I shot every bullet. They weren't going to run me out if powder and lead would stop them.

"And my Johnny didn't miss a day of school."

Not only did this amazing woman get her Johnny Mack through high school, she got him through college.

"I had been pinching off a little penny here and a little penny there for his graduation trip because there wasn't anything that was going to keep me away.

"Then some white folks I had worked for gave me some

money for the trip. And then some more money came along and I ended up with enough for the trip and a nice present for Johnny Mack.

"And then before I left some of my white and colored friends got together and got me a Cadillac to ride in to Greensboro for that boy's graduation.

"I was as happy as I could be to see that boy graduate. That just proves that everytime I did something for someone else I gained something."

But her work wasn't finished.

There was the matter of the weed-choked lot where the winos threw their bottles. She got that cleaned off and today it stands officially as "Mattie's Mini Park."

Then there were the streets in her part of town.

"The town had the money allocated for them and they spent it in the white part of town and told the colored children they had to walk since the street here was too rough to drive the bus on.

"Now it's paved."

But probably her most lasting accomplishments are the bathrooms.

The project began when the town got some federal funds.

"Most of these old houses down here by the creek didn't have indoor bathrooms. Those old people had to haul their pails down to the creek and empty them. We got a committee up to see how to spend the money and give them names of people. We made sure the bathrooms didn't go in rental houses owned by other people.

"There were so many people who lived in Grifton all their lives and wore themselves out for this town and they couldn't afford to put in bathrooms.

"When you're living on Social Security you do good just to live. Now they've got their bathrooms indoors at least."

Mrs. Mattie Dixon. We're all better because of her.

Melvin Whitehead, Trucker

Washington.

We watched as the girl with the bottled hair walked away, her sweat-stained waitress dress a size too small.

"That's her right there," Mel said. "That's the good-looking truck stop waitress everybody talks about. Nice, ain't she?"

No, she wasn't. But then many of them aren't. Girls with pretty faces find better jobs than pouring coffee in a roadside cafe that smells old.

Mel didn't look like a trucker, or maybe he did. We've been lied to often enough that we believe the trucker is the last American cowboy, a restless soul that pushes his fire-belching rig from coast to coast and back again, running from speed traps and chasing a dream.

In our plastic, look-alike world, the trucker is real.

I was sharing a counter with Melvin Whitehead from Orlando, Fla. I wanted coffee and he wanted to talk. The cab of a shaking semi can be a lonely place.

"Sometimes it ain't so bad," he said. "When the weather is good and the traffic is light, you can move right along. But when it rains and your head hurts and you're losing time — man, it can be hell.

"That's what they don't show in them movies. They don't show you trying to sleep in the cab while you wait for the warehouse to open.

"They don't show you arguing with your wife when she wants to go on vacation and the last thing you want to do is go anywhere.

"They don't show you trying to get up to drive the same load up the same road for the two-hundreth time.

"They don't show you missing your kids."

Nobody makes Mel drive a truck. He's been doing it for 23 years now, making good money but not having the energy or the time to spend it. He does it because he's always done it and that's all he knows.

He is a trucker and a trucker drives trucks. They don't sell shoes.

"Some of these boys believe all that stuff and they like being cowboys," he says, nodding at a trio of booted drivers nearby. "Look at them cowboy boots. Now what good is a pair of cowboy boots in a truck? But it makes them happy, so what the hell.

"They'll learn. I used to be like that. I'd flirt with waitresses and race with other trucks. But not anymore.

"Now all I want to do is get home again in one piece.

"I don't want to eat in no more truck stops. I don't want to drive through 24 hours of rain and headlights. I don't want to hear that damn old CB radio in my ears. I try to drive and not think about it.

"But every now and then, when it's going good and the traffic is light, it's a helluva feeling to be sitting up there and watching that big old road coming at you.

"Jeez, will you look at that?" Mel said, nodding toward the oily rainbow on the cooling coffee in front of us.

"I ain't never seen that in no movie."

Duck Sykes, General Merchandise

Spring Hope.

Albert Bunn left his mark in Spring Hope, right there on the side of Duck Sykes's rolltop desk.

"Old man Bunn used to come down here every day to sit by the coal stove," Duck said, as we stood in the friendly shadows of the Sykes Seed Store. "It don't matter how hot that fire got, Mr. Bunn wouldn't move, sitting right there in the corner with his head leaning back on the desk. To this day you can see the imprint of his head. His children come in here every time they come back to visit to rub their hands over the mark his head made."

That's the way life has always been at Sykes Seed Store, at 78, the oldest business in Spring Hope. And it is still exactly like that.

"You don't see places like this anymore," Duck said. "This place is the same way it was when my father opened it up 78 years ago. I'll sweep the floor, but that's all. People wouldn't want me to change it."

This is one of those stores where if you can't think of where to buy something, you go see Duck Sykes, he probably has it ... somewhere. You may have to move things around, but it's there.

There is a certain lovely logic to the arrangement of things here, but it escapes me.

One counter back by the heater is arranged as follows:

freezer bags, cast iron frying pans, fireplace andirons, dog food, sugar, flour and "thunder mugs." And that's on the front side of one shelf. Lord only knows what's on the back side, but I did spot a shiny brass kettle next to the detergent next to a case of 2,500 books of matches.

In one glass-front display case up front are screw drivers, butcher knives, work gloves, two kinds of suspenders (with and without buttons), shoe laces and women's hosiery and all that is within reach of a case with mops, safety pins, aspirin, glue, flashlights, thermometers, red and blue handkerchiefs, BBs and shoe polish.

"Of course I know where everything is," Duck thundered. I think I'd insulted him. "And if there is a dead item, something that doesn't move in here, I don't know what it is."

This high-ceilinged, cane chair, spit box, unevened floor, cooled by nature general store, with peeling wall posters advertising Arbuckle Coffee ("America's favorite for over 60 years" and formerly a big seller), Moon Shine tobacco and Red Seal Lye ("Best Soap Maker"), has been home to Duck Sykes all his 72 years, except for World War II.

"I was in Louisiana, and they asked for volunteers for the 82nd Airborne Division," he said. "Then they told me I'd go to Fort Bragg and that was good enough for me."

After the war — his war stories of the Normandy invasion and Nijmegen assault in flimsy gliders where he held out for 28 days surrounded by Germans are hair-raising indeed — Duck Sykes came home.

The good folks of Spring Hope were glad to see Duck when he came home from the war. Duck was known far and wide as something of a hunter ("That airborne training wasn't nothing for me, I'd been running through these woods all my life") and, when he left to go off and whip the Germans, his passel of hunting dogs were farmed out to neighbors for the duration.

"They knew I was coming home, so everybody brought all the dogs back to the pen behind the store," he laughed. "When I walked to that pen every one of them dogs knew who I was, although one of them had mourned to death. I let them all out and went home from here, them dogs going with me, just a'barking and raising hell.

"Everybody spread the word, Duck Sykes was home and everybody was glad of it, especially me.

"When that bus crossed the railroad tracks, I swore I wouldn't ever get over one meal away from here, and I've done my best to live up to that promise," he said. "We might take us a little trip now and then, but not too far away.

"Spring Hope is good enough for me."

But before we leave Duck Sykes, why is he called Duck since his name is actually Johnny?

"When I was a kid everybody had a nickname," he said. "There was Red and Sparrow, a little fellow, and my name ended up as Duck. Could be worse, though.

"My brother's name is Frog."

Cora Mae Basnight, Actress

Manteo.

"I competed with a bunch of those pretty college girls," Cora Mae Basnight said with a whoop. "They didn't have a chance. Pretty faces are a dime a dozen but faces like mine stand out.

"Every time a photographer comes by, all those pretty little girls start primping. I tell them to forget it, he's coming to take my picture."

For 24 years Cora Mae Basnight has been going one-on-one with pretty girls trying out for parts in "The Lost Colony," and every year the director has chosen this 69-year-old native Roanoke Islander for the coveted role of Agona, the mute Indian squaw who spends most of the show chasing her true love, the colonist named Old Tom.

"Those pretty queens and handsome young men playing Sir Walter Raleigh come and go, but old Agona hangs on," she said with a laugh. "With a face like this and a character like that, I'm the one they remember. When they ask a pretty girl for her autograph, they're flirting. When they ask for mine, they're sincere."

The cast and crew have honored her with a distinguished service award. She has been in the show longer than anyone else, and there is talk that she has been playing her part longer than any other actor or actress in any outdoor drama in the country.

She lives in one of those breezy, rambling old houses in Manteo, the kind of place where on any given day you're likely to find one or more of her children or grandchildren romping through.

We sat on her wrap-around porch just killing time and letting the world roll past.

"I've stuck with the show because I love it," she said. "After my divorce, I said, 'Well, pshaw, it's time for me to get goin' and now every night is like the beginning.

"When I stand backstage, I can look out across the sound to the Wright Brothers monument and it is lovely to me. We've got a mama duck and nine little ones living back there now, and it is a beautiful place to be.

"They'll have to carry me out of there on a stretcher to get rid of me. I was sick one time and had to miss some performances, so I went and watched my understudy do it. She was rotten, twittering around like a teen-ager. It was awful, I couldn't stand it.

"Every year somebody wants to play my part. Well, they can forget it. I'll be back. After I was gone that time, I came back and gave it a little extra. They knew Cora Mae Basnight was back."

Except for a brief time when she lived in the mountains with her husband, Mrs. Basnight has always lived on the island, and she is here to stay, even when the fearsome Atlantic hurricanes roar in.

"I've never left in a storm," she said. "My God, no. I want to be in the middle of it. I don't want to miss anything.

"Let 'er blow. If she takes me, I'll go. That's the best way for an Islander to go anyway. You live by the sea and you die by the sea. There is something about the wind and the sea that I love.

"Every morning I get up and look out my window. I can see the water and the earth.

"I don't go to church all the time — just enough so they'll know who I am. It helps if you have somebody to preach your funeral — but no preacher can give me what I can get from the sea and the earth. That's my heaven."

Working with the youthful cast of the show, year after year, she is in an excellent position to observe the young, and she likes what she sees.

"They're just like we were," she said, laughing, "but a lot of people forget that. They have pot, and we had white lightning. Both are illegal.

"There were five bootleggers in Manteo when I was young. One ran a filling station, and you could get both ends gassed up. I rode with the bootleggers many a time.

"I understand these young people. I think I'm broad-minded enough to accept it. I know good and well that if there had been pot around when we were young, we'd have tried it, too.

"Our fun was different. We might steal a chicken or a watermelon, and have to climb out of the window to sneak out at night, but there isn't much real difference in people.

"The one thing I can't ever be is holier than thou.

"I've had a good time with my life, how in the world could I ever have any regrets?"

Willie B. Hopkins, Mr. Everything

Zebulon.

He is a giant of a man.

Standing six feet, five inches tall and weighing in at 265 pounds, this gentle man would wade unarmed into the roughest honky tonk in town, grab a drunk in each hand and drag them five blocks to jail.

The next day he would go out to a widow's house and wring a chicken's neck because she couldn't bear to.

And there are still times when he reads a letter to a friend who can't.

It is good that Willie B. Hopkins is so big, because for 40 years he has carried a town on his broad shoulders.

Willie B., as he's known here, first adopted Zebulon in December 1937 when he was hired as the town constable.

Between then and 1977, when he retired, he had been a policeman, the police chief, fire chief, town manager, clerk, treasurer, street superintendent, tax collector, superintendent of the water and sewer systems, the sanitation supervisor, building inspector, clerk of Recorders Court, electrical inspector, reader of water meters, street designer, ditch digger and water and sewer line installer, a radio personality and the best friend this Wake

County town ever had.

He didn't do those jobs one at a time. He did them all at once. For nearly 40 years he was Zebulon.

"I've had lots of opportunities to leave, but I knew how to operate here," he said as he showed me his town. "I knew what my limits were.

"I've always operated under the theory that you ought not to get higher on the totem pole than you can stay."

He began as a policeman, working 12 hours a day, seven days a week, 365 days a year, plus overtime.

Along came the war and help got hard to find, so Police Officer Hopkins became Everything Hopkins. He kept on doing it when the war was over because, simply, he knew how.

"I couldn't get sick. I didn't have the time," he says, and those are not the words of a braggart. That's just the way he feels about Zebulon. He got some help later on, but he was still in charge of everything.

Some thoughts on his career:

"I used to have to make the budget and collect the taxes, too. It makes you more serious about it when you have to go out and get the money you're spending."

"The joints used to be a lot easier to control. I'd go in and tell a drunk to go home and he did. Now they'd shoot you. I didn't have a police car so I either had to shuffle them off to jail or convince them to walk. I'd do it however they wanted it."

"Up until 10 years ago I could have called the name of every human being in town. And I believe they could have called mine."

"My daddy told me that if someone was willing to pay me $65 to work for the town that I should stick with it. I did."

Finally in 1971 cancer tried to kill him. It got an eye, but he was too tough.

"They finally hired me an assistant then and I've been training him real good so he's ready now," he says, smiling. "Hell, I wouldn't quit if he wasn't."

"They tell me it's time to go, and I guess it is, but I still hope to make some contributions, to help Zebulon some.

"I'm satisfied as I could be, I guess, but still ..."

The words begin to come hard. The big man has been here too long to walk away without looking back. The big man also has a soft heart.

"But you can tell them all they haven't seen the last of Willie B. Hopkins.

"I'll be back."

Godspeed, Willie B.

Susie, Sherry and Ronda

White Lake.

Let's see if I have this straight.

They live in Wallace, at least two of them work in Burgaw, they go to school at Wallace-Rose Hill High School, which isn't in Wallace or Rose Hill at all but is really in Teachey, they like the boys in Burgaw and go to either Wilmington or White Lake to have fun.

I think that's right, but when you talk to Susie and Sherry Gurgainous and Ronda Lane, it is hard enough to remember where you are, much less keep up with the details.

I ran into this Terrific Trio when I was tryings to get out of the rain and they were riding the merry-go-round, which everyone knows is really called the hobby horses.

I tried to ignore them at first, but when three good looking girls scream at me in unison, well, I gave in to temptation.

"Take my picture. Take my picture," they yelled, almost falling off the hobby horses in their exuberance. They waved, threw their legs in the air, and generally acted like well-behaved teen-agers while trying to get my attention.

What was I to do but oblige?

Susie is 18 and is the sister of Sherry, who is 17. I tried to tell Ronda she was supposed to spell her name with an 'h' but she wouldn't listen. Teen-agers never pay attention to their elders. Anyway, Ronda is 17 and is a friend of Susie and Sherry.

I remember asking them what they were doing here. They never did tell me, or maybe they just never got around to it. Or maybe they did, and I don't remember.

But I did learn that Susie pumps gas and sells beer at

her father's Citgo station.

"When they come to our station to get gassed up, we really gas 'em up," she said.

As is inevitable when talking to teen-age girls, the subject of boys is upppermost.

"You know what's funny?" Ronda said. It wasn't really a question. "Some guy will wear a Farrah Fawcett T-shirt, the one with her in a BATHING SUIT (Ronda is the only person I know who speaks in capital letters), and he will wear it on a date with a brunette.

"But I don't worry about her. She's not real. But he's cute."

He who? I was having trouble with this gang.

"The guy running the hobby horses," she said, turning to leer. "Hey you, good looking, can we ride for nothing?"

"Good Looking" looked okay, if you go in for those suntanned, muscular types with tousled hair, but he was clearly uneasy with this gang. I knew how he felt.

"Now don't go telling him he's good looking" Sherry said. "He'll have a big head over it. But he is."

How about the boys in Wallace, I asked.

"The good looking ones are in Burgaw," Susie said. "A lot of the boys in Wallace are scody."

Scody?

"You know, scaggy."

Oh.

What is there to do in Wallace on a good-time Saturday night?

"Go to Burgaw," Susie said. "But if you stay there you go park your cars in a big circle in the Piggly Wiggly parking lot and rap. Then you see who is riding up and down the four lane and who leaves with whom and when they come back. Then you see if there is mud on the car so you'll know where they went."

We said goodby, they to hustle another ride on the merry-go-round and me to nurse my addled brain.

"You know," one of them said, "you look younger than your picture."

Thanks a lot, girls.

Robert McAdams, Mule Farmer

Wilson.
What more could a man need?

A woodburning stove, a mule, two hogs, 20 chickens, two dogs, an old farmhouse, four acres of land, an outhouse and a $2.95 electricity bill should be enough for anyone.

It is for Robert McAdams, college graduate and artist.

"Some people might think I'm living in poverty," he says. "But poverty is a state of mind.

"And most people think I've left the rat race. That's not so. I've only left their rat race for my own. I'm just not a slave to cars and houses like they are."

For six years now McAdams, 28, has been living the life of the old-timey farmer. He gets up at 5 a.m., hitches Sister, the One-Eyed Mule, to a plow and works his vegetables as long as the light holds.

The only difference is that during the day he leaves for a few hours to teach art in the Wilson County school system.

"That old mule of mine is the most hooked and unhooked mule in the world," he says.

McAdams, city born and bred, decided while he was in college that there was something about the land that called him, something that made him want to chunk his thoroughly average suburban life-style and get his hands dirty.

He began by learning: "I knew I didn't know anything about it, so I went all over Wilson County looking for a mule farmer who would let me apprentice with him. I worked and learned everything I could."

Finally his chance came. His mentor, Moses Godwin, leased him eight acres and he went to work on his own.

"I was there five years and almost all of it was done by hand," he said. "My family helped some, and I had to hire hands to put in tobacco, and the first year I made exactly $56, but I proved I could do it and make a profit."

Now it is vegetables. He raises mustard greens, cabbage, potatoes, cucumbers, squash, butter beans, peas and corn on his neatly plowed rows, loading up his old pickup at picking time and hauling his produce to local stores.

"To me this is not an agribusiness, it is a life-style," he said. "I get up in the morning and look out the window and I know what my life will be that day.

"I get my living and all my food, so what more do I need? I've got my hogs and my eggs and last year I canned 235 jars of food. If your values are in money, then don't farm like this, but self-sufficiency is important to me.

"I could have bought a tractor and all that equipment, but man is in too big a hurry now. You need some time to think things out, and when you're looking at the back end of a mule all day there is not much else to do but think."

His farm on Hog Island Road (officially it's Firestone Boulevard) is a friendly place. Dusty, the bad-mannered dog, chases a rooster. Sister wanders out to have her ears rubbed. The hogs grunt contentedly, not knowing what awaits them when the weather gets cold.

It is peaceful listening to him talk of dirt and cutting his own firewood with a one-man crosscut saw. The big trees lull you into believing that maybe this is the way it ought to be.

"But you know, folks won't let you work," Robert says. "I was getting along fine with my saw, but my folks insisted on giving me a chain saw.

"I'll tell you what made me the happiest, though. It was moving to this house where I had a pump on the back porch. Now that's mighty convenient. My last one was in the yard.

"I feel like I've come up in the world."

Oswald Singer, Legionnaire

Morehead City.

Oswald Singer remembers the day in 1939 when he marched off to join a legend.

He was an Austrian Jew, on the run from Hitler and the Gestapo. They had missed him by mere days in Vienna. He lied his way out of Germany. They didn't catch him when Gestapo agents searched him at the border; he kept moving, living by his wits.

He was living in Paris, illegally selling English-language newspapers to stay alive, trying to dodge French detectives who scoured the streets for refugees who tried to work.

The rules were simple: Stay invisible and when confronted, keep talking, keep smiling and keep moving.

"But I wanted to fight Hitler so I went down to join the French Army," Singer said. "They told me I could join their 'Legion of Foreigners' and I asked if that was the French Foreign Legion.

"They said it wasn't, that it was a unit of foreigners who would be trained and then assigned to regular French units. I still didn't know what was happening until I walked in the barracks and saw that slogan. I'll never forget it."

There were three words, the motto of "the greatest collection of cutthroats, perverts, murderers and criminals from all over the world," Singer said.

"March Or Die." Welcome to the French Foreign Legion and saddle up for the Sahara.

"There were men there from all over the world, even Nazi spies," Singer remembers of those grueling days in the wasteland of the world. "I wrote a letter to my brother that there were Nazis in my unit, but of course they censored the mail.

"I was ordered before the commander and sentenced to eight days in prison for writing there were Nazis in the legion. I refused to name them, but when I got to prison they had already been picked up and were waiting for me. If I had broken my silence, can you imagine what would have happened to a Jew in prison with Nazis? They knew I hadn't named them so I had no trouble. They called me 'The Preacher.' One day they even raised the Nazi flag instead of the French flag, that's how many of them there were."

But trouble was coming, big trouble. France fell to Germany, and the foreigners in the legion were asked where they wanted to go now that the war was over for them. Singer asked for America.

He got slave labor in the Sahara.

"Instead of discharging us as they said they were doing, the Vichy government rented us to the Trans-Sahara Railroad Company to build a railroad from Morocco to Algeria," Singer recalled. "But we were paid. Exactly one cent per day."

The railroad was laid on a bed of stone 21 feet high.

That bed of stone was built by slave legionnaires, with sho-vels and sweat. Singer's job was to crack large boulders into smaller ones, and then the smaller ones into gravel.

The food was soup, usually of wormy lentils. The temperature soared above 100 during the day, below freezing at night. The men who had joined the legendary French Foreign Legion to fight for freedom lived in holes in the ground.

Some legionnaires even agreed to join Rommel in the Afrika Corps to escape, but not Singer or the 40 Jews in his camp. They kept insisting they had the right to be free men, and Singer remembers the day a French officer came to inspect them. Singer stood in formation, singing, "Anyone can see what's troubling me, I'm crying for my liberty."

That can get a man in trouble anywhere, and after Singer and his Jewish comrades held an illegal religious cere-mony, Singer was sent to the tombs.

"Tombeau" (the tomb) was a prison at Ain El Ourak in the Sahara. It was often a one-way trip. For eight days Singer lived in a hole with the sun bearing down. A cup of water, a piece of bread and the sun, always the sun. And at night there was the cold.

Finally Americans and British forces arrived and Singer was freed. By 1947 he had made his way to America where now he says simply:

"Nothing can happen to me now. For so long I was a man without a country, now I'm an American."

Sam Jenkins, Healer

Walstonburg.

Sam Jenkins really wanted to be a doctor, so it was only natural that in 1926 when he came here as the town's only druggist, he did what he could to help out.

"We only had one doctor in town then and he was hard of hearing," Jenkins said, standing in the lonely shadows that used to be his combination drug and general mercan-tile store.

"He had more than he could do, so I had to help. You fill enough prescriptions and ask enough questions and you learn a lot.

"Times were so hard then that people didn't have

enough money to pay a doctor, so I've picked many a cotton seed out of an ear or many a cockle burr out of a nose.

"I stayed busy lancing boils and I've pulled many a loose tooth sitting right here in my office. I guess I've done everything from deliver babies on up.

"All in all, I was just a poor man's doctor."

That's the way it was back then. Many of us can remember being pulled into a drugstore to stand in front of that high counter while our mothers patiently explained to the man in the white coat what was wrong and please, wasn't there something he could do to make it better.

The numbing terror of the Depression came shortly after Jenkins opened his drug store here.

"People still got sick whether they had enough money to pay for it or not," he said. "I sold medicine right on regardless of whether I got paid or not.

"And in 50 years I never had a bad debt over $400."

There are still mementoes galore in the old drugstore. A collection of medicine bottles that were there when he bought the store line the dusty shelves, many of then containing the original drugs.

"We didn't just open a bottle and pour pills into another bottle and put a label on it in those days," he said. "We mixed everything, by hand, ourselves.

"And you see that bottle? That's the bottle of perfume I used to wear when I went courting."

The smell-good is called "Honolulu Bouquet" and all I can say is it's a wonder he ever got married.

"And those bottles there are peach and apple flavoring I used to sell by the case to mix with Monkey Rum (I call it moonshine). You put a pint bottle of that to a gallon of Monkey Rum and it tastes just like it came from a store.

"We used to open at 7 a.m. and we'd go home toward bedtime, say around 9 or 10 o'clock. If I didn't stay, there was nobody to do it.

"Now don't you go getting me in trouble with the doctors for telling you all this."

I don't think they'll mind, Doc Jenkins. If it hadn't been for the men like you in the white jackets behind tall counters in a hundred small towns, a lot of us, including some doctors, might not be here today.

Jenkins packed his mortar and pestle away last year, but not because he wanted to: "I had seven robberies last year and after the last one I closed. I couldn't keep drugs.

"It was like losing a member of the family."

But not everyone got the word that Doc Jenkins was out of the healing business.

"Just today a man came in who had mashed his finger about off and he wanted me to take care of it.

"So I did."

Russell Powell, Music Man

Southern Pines. "What this is, you see, is Southern Pine's version of your country service station where the boys come to drink a little beer, tell a few lies and pick some music," Russell Powell said.

Lord knows it has all the trimmings. First of all there is Powell, certified by all in this golfing resort as the official village character. He said he is the "Mayor of Pinedene." Others say he is just old weird Russ.

The first thing you notice when you come in the door of the Pinedene Jazz Center is Powell propped up in the corner, a one-legged, slimmed-down version of Burl Ives. Don't worry about the leg. As his friend Glenn Rounds said, "Now he can tie his shoes in half the time." That makes Russ laugh.

There will be a mandolin within arm's reach. And if you stay, and if Russ and his band of hangers-on don't think you're too much of a jerk, he is likely to pick up the mandolin and knock your ears off with jazz as you've never heard it before.

And while they're playing, you can look around the cluttered shop. It is, at heart, a music store. But then you notice the signs.

Stuff like, "Your money cheerfully refunded if not satisfactory. So far, all your money has been satisfactory."

About then, Russ and his sideman, this day it was employee Bob Hensley on guitar, will change into a bouncy John Philip Sousa march while you read the sign that says

"Recessions don't bother me, I was a failure during prosperity."

It is safe to say that just about everyone here knows and likes Russ Powell. Who else could get away with having a "Going back into business sale" with prices raised anywhere from 25 to 80 percent for one week only and run an advertisement in the local paper ... and get away with it.

Who else could get away with having the annual Biggest SOB in Southern Pines election (Russ claims it means Sweet Old Boy, but Russ lies about things like that)?

"Sometimes we have 40 or 50 candidates," Russ said, and when I said I didn't know there were that many deserving SOBs in Southern Pines, he added, "Well, you ain't lived here for 50 years either."

And who else could run newspaper advertisements each Christmas that say "Bah, Humbug"? Folks in Southern Pines don't think it is Christmas until Russ's ads appear.

The Pinedene Jazz Center is the home, or lair, of the Pinedene Symphony, a loosely knit group at best. But they are also some of the best musicians around, folks who like to come down and sit in with Russ and whomever else shows up. They have even made personal appearances, at places like hospitals.

At 60, Russ is one of the few natives here. He spent his childhood working with his father in their combination service station and grocery store and one day picked up a mandolin.

"We had us a Billy Carter-style service station. We sold beer, drank bourbon and raised hell," Russ said.

And if Billy Carter ran a music store, this is the store he would run.

But when the jokes end and the music starts, you quickly realize that Russ Powell is good, very good. He switches easily from jazz to 1940s Big Band tunes to marches to classical music to Italian songs. I asked him why he never tried to make it big.

"There is nothing but frustration anywhere else but at the top," he said seriously. "And at the top, there's a killing grind.

"Frankly, I'm too lazy. I don't like to practice, I like to

play. And there is a big difference.''

And play he does, every day. Sometimes just with Bob, who when he looks at Russ and Russ isn't looking back, has awe in his eyes. Bob ain't no slouch on guitar, but Russ is that good.

''When I'm at home with nothing going on, there is music in my head, it is with me all the time,'' Russ said. ''I cannot imagine anyone going through life without an instrument.''

But the advertisement he once ran in the paper, under the heading ''The Pinedene Report'' puts it best, sort of brings Russ Powell and his two-sided love affair with this town in perspective:

''Russell Powell claims he has charisma.

''Russell Powell claims he has machismo.

''Russell Powell claims he is suave and debonair.

''Russell Powell claims he is the world's greatest mandolin player.

''Russell Powell's friends claim he is the world's greatest liar.''

There would be a Southern Pines without Russ, and there would be a music store, but as Bob Hensley said,''There wouldn't be the same quantity, or quality, of crazies here without him.''

Louise Anderson, Storyteller

Jacksonville.

The old man would have been proud of the little girl who used to sit on his front porch and listen to the tales he would tell.

It was on Eccles Street in High Point and Lee Sims was the neighborhood storyteller.

''He used to tell us the scariest stories,'' Louise Anderson said. ''They were always ghost stories. You'd be afraid to wash your feet and go to bed. Everybody I knew had at least one experience with a ghost after listening to him.''

Now the tradition continues. Story telling, the oldest form of literature we have, lives in the heart of this wonderfully happy woman.

"My people have always told stories," she said in her mother's home here, while outside a steady spring rain dropped a gray curtain to hide the real world and I became lost in the legends of Shiney and a pony named Sammy Racer and the evils that would befall you if you dared mix watermelon and whiskey.

"I used to tell stories 20 years ago when I babysat white children at a church," Ms. Anderson said. "They'd keep quiet when I told them a story."

Her love for stories and black poetry continued, through job after job, until last year when a federal grant made it possible for the Onslow County Library to hire her as a full-time teller of tall tales. Now that the grant has ended, she is doing it on her own, full time, a professional storyteller.

"Most of the stories I tell are ones I remember from my childhood, ones I heard from my mother or from Mr. Sims, but I do make some of them up myself," she said. "And there are those marvelous (works by) old black preachers and black poets."

Ms. Anderson' tales delve into the black experience, seeking literary beginnings, but always tinged with love and humor. Listening to her get wound up will raise goose-bumps. Her delivery impassioned, the spell captivating.

"Most of those old stories and games went from plantation to plantation and they survived the slavery days," she said. "New York was named 'The Big Apple' because a man going through South Carolina saw some black children playing a singing game. He took them to New York to show it off and soon everybody in New York was doing 'The Big Apple.' "

African legends about Anansi the Spider Man survived the slaver's chains, got changed to "Aunt Nancy" by whites who couldn't understand the black dialect and ended up as the foundation for those marvelous "Uncle Remus" stories.

During 1976 Ms. Anderson and the rest of her talented family put on a black entertainment called, "It's Time to Tell The Children," a collection of the old songs, stories and games. They toured it through the East. Much of that show lives in her performance now.

And add to that the powerful sermons of James Weldon

Johnson and the gripping poetry of Langston Hughes ("The Negro Mother") and you have Louise Anderson, storyteller.

A Jaci Early poem she loves pretty much sums up this lady:

"Got up this morning feeling good and black,
Thinking black thoughts,
Played all my black records,
And minded my own black business,
Put on my best black clothes,
Walked out my black door,
And Lord have mercy,
White snow."

"Sammy Racer," her most famous story, was recently published, with characters the likes of Garden Eden Slick, the platform shoe-wearing, jive-talking snake; Kareem J. MacAdoo, the basketball-playing giraffe; O. J. Too Bad Namath, a gorilla who plays football; Muhammed A. Spinkeroo, the boxing kangaroo; Ms. Farrah Lindsay Fa Lana, a foxy fox; and last but far from least, the regal King Abraham Carter Washington.

It ends with these lovely lines, "For if anything is once loved with a love that is true, that thing shall everlastingly belong to you."

That says a lot about Louise Anderson and her stories.

Paula Marie Duncan, Valedictorian

Culbreth.
There is one in every school.

A quiet person who makes the best grades, seemingly without effort, but someone who seems different somehow.

They are there when the awards are handed out, but never when trouble breaks out.

They seem to glide through school in a mystical haze, known by many, but friends with few.

They are treasured by teachers and parents, but for classmates, well, that is another story.

Sometimes the story is painful. School for some people can be a lonely place.

Her name is Paula Marie Duncan, valedictorian of the

1977 graduating class of South Granville High School.

"Being a Christian and following Christ in the public schools can be hard," Paula said in her farmhouse living room in this community near Oxford. "You have to decide whether to follow Christ or the group. Peer pressure is awfully hard.

"For awhile I withdrew and I'd criticize people who treated me badly, but only within myself. But I came to realize that if there were differences in me and them, and there always will be, I'd try to enjoy being with them without giving up what I know is right just for a relationship."

There was teasing, some of it cruel. Since she had never made anything but straight A's since the fourth grade, and moved to the school from Maryland four years ago, and was a professed Christian, it was easy for the closeknit society of country folks to look at her as someone from "out there," someone not to be entirely trusted.

Part of it she brought on herself, she admits.

"I can't stand cheating," she said. "I abhor it. Teachers weren't doing anything, but if I see it and don't do anything about it, it's like I'm condoning it.

"One time I had to turn in my best friend for cheating. That's one time I felt like people were talking about me and it hurt.

"He asked me if I'd turned him in and I said yes. He didn't talk to me for a long time, but now we're great friends.

"I feel like I work and study for what I get and it doesn't seem fair for them to cheat. Sometimes I feel guilty about doing it, but in the end I'm glad I've done it. A lot of times I have to think about it and my feelings go against it, but I knew it was the right thing to do.

"It wasn't always a lot of fun to be in school. People who had been the tops in the class when I got here suddenly weren't anymore. Some of them became my friends, but a lot of them didn't care much for me.

"I didn't date very much in school because no one asked me. But I'd hear about the things they did on weekends and frankly I didn't want to have anything to do with that.

"But my peer group was more important to me than I

wanted to admit sometimes. And it wasn't fun when things were going on and I was left out. I did feel alone, uncomfortable and strange sometimes, but I feel better off because I did.

"At first I wanted to force my standards on them, but I know now I can't. They came to know what I stand for and I know them.

"I probably spend more time with my family than other people my age, but I think that's good.

"But there always was that little feeling that I was being left out, that I was missing something.

"There were things in my church, though, that helped make up for it and I have no regrets for the way I live my life."

Rex Whitehurst, Daredevil

Jacksonville

Five years ago Rex Whitehurst was broke.

"I told a guy in Texas I'd jump my motorcycle over six cars for $50," he remembered. "It was a total disaster. It cost me $400 in hospital bills, four months in a cast and I destroyed my motorcycle.

"I laid there in bed thinking this sure wasn't for me."

But then a man in Atlanta paid Rex Whitehurst to jump his motorcycle again, this time over 15 buses. And this time he got $50,000.

"Wreckless Rex" Whitehurst has arrived.

He is now a full-fledged daredevil, a Jacksonville boy who has jumped his motorcycle farther than anyone in history, even eclipsing Evel Knievel.

He does it, he claims, "only for the money."

"I was a poor boy. We used to have to buy six drinks and split them among nine of us kids.

"I didn't get much education and I worked and worked but I couldn't get nowhere. I was tired of being poor, so I got a motorcycle.

"I used to have to get a loan to buy a set of tires for my car. Now I can buy me a set of tires if I want to and I don't need no damn bankers to loan me the money.

"I won't never be poor no more if I can help it."

Whitehurst's battle to escape the soul-numbing poverty of his early life has been costly. He has broken bones and left a lot of skin on cheap tracks all over the country, thrilling people and hustling a buck.

But the money, and he has made some good money, won't buy off the fear, the terror that grabs his gut before every jump.

"The last hour is the worst," he said as we sipped tea in a steak house the other day. "Everything is ready and there is nothing to do but wait.

"I know that half the people are there hoping I'll get killed. My crew says they've heard people yelling they hope I splatter and bust my head and some of them actually boo when I make it.

"But they paid $5 apiece to be there and for $5 a man can say anything he wants of me. I don't care, as long as I get paid.

"But once I get on that bike and crank it up all the pressure is gone. It's like pulling a sore tooth. I'm still scared as hell, but I wouldn't have the nerve not to jump. I couldn't face the ridicule.

"You know that feeling you get the first time you jump off a high diving board? Well that's what I feel every time I jump.

"I won't ever do anything I know will kill me, but I'll go to the limit. There ain't enough money for me to die, but getting hurt? I'll take that chance for money."

But in spite of his supposed greed and love for money, there is more to it, something besides the money. Because a man who does it only for the money would be equally willing not to do it if someone would pay him.

"I hadn't thought about it that way," he said. "But no, nobody could pay me not to jump. And if somebody else jumps further than I do, well, I'll have to jump further than he does, I guess.

"Evel Knievel will always be number one, but I'm going to be number two.

And what happens when it's over, when no one is willing to pay to see a man risk his life making a motorcycle do something it isn't meant to do? What happens when the possibility of death bores us?

"I'm good for two more years," he said. "And I want to make enough money to buy me a McDonalds hamburger place and hire somebody to run it.

"I don't ever plan to work again. And I don't plan to be poor again, either."

Capt. Fred Gillikin, Lifesaver

Morehead City.

The year that Capt. Fred Gillikin first knew life, the nation's first commercial telephone exchange went into operation.

The next year, F. W. Woolworth opened the nation's first 5- and 10-cent store.

He was 8 years old when Geronimo surrendered, 17 when X-rays were discovered, and by the time the Wright Brothers first flew an airplane, Capt. Fred had already finished his first hitch in the Coast Guard and was a married man.

Capt. Fred, as those of us lucky enough to know him call him, is what leprechauns grow up to be: twinkling, charming men with lightning wits and quicker minds.

Capt. Fred Gillikin is 100 years old — enough to make him the oldest living U.S. Coast Guard veteran in the world. In fact, he is even older than the Coast Guard, harkening back to the days of the old Lifesaving Service.

"I'm ready to go right now," Capt. Fred said. "If the Coast Guard needs me, I'm ready.

"I'm known as a Coast Guard man and I've never fought that. The majority of retirees are just waiting for their checks, but I'm a real Coast Guard man. It's my life. It's in here," he said, thumping his solid chest and beaming. I'd serve with Capt. Fred tomorrow if he'd take me on his crew.

"I grew up in a boat," he said of his pre-1900 days as a wind sailor, days spent dredging for oysters, hauling produce up to Norfolk, anything to get along.

"I've never been afraid in a boat, never, not once."

There were times when lesser men would have been afraid. Like the time he bossed the very first rescue ever by the U. S. Coast Guard.

"On the 17th of March in 1915, at six o'clock in the morning, we sighted a three-masted schooner standing on Cape Lookout Shoals in a terrible storm," he said. "The sea was awful rough. We ate us a mouthful of breakfast and then boarded the open lifeboat.

"She (the Sylvia C. Hall) was 10 miles out there and had breakers coming all over her, all the way over her crosstrees and that must have been 75 feet high.

"We couldn't get in close to her and just before night my bosun's mate said, 'Captain, let's go in. We'll all die out here tonight.'

"It was a hard thing to do, going in and leaving those men out there. It was a terrible time.

"But we went in, got some food and took out another self-bailing boat. We left two men on the shore to save us if we needed them. This time we got in close enough for the crew to lower themselves from the jib boom, and we picked up all five of them. Didn't lose a man.

"What do you think of my memory now?" he asked, grinning because he knew what I'd been thinking. After all, he is a hundred.

Capt. Fred once told a friend that he was pleased he had lived so long, "but the thing I like the best is that the Lord let me keep my mind."

On Capt. Fred's 100th birthday, the people of Morehead City said thanks. The Coast Guard sent up a 378-foot-long cutter for the day; a parade with 40 units marched past Capt. Fred; there was a big ball at a local nightspot — all for the man who may have saved their grandfather's life.

Now he spends his days in a marvelous old coastal home in his beloved Marshallburg, living with his 78-year-old baby daughter, the even more spry and feisty Mrs. Iva Fisher.

"She got mad at me last year," Capt. Fred said. "I went up on the roof (three stories high) to work on the TV antenna.

"Of course, I was only 99 then, not a hundred like I am now."

Happy Birthday, Capt. Fred Gillikin, and, for all of us, thank you.

Capt. Gillikin died July 13, 1978.

Bobby Wilkerson, Ugly

Henderson.

I'll tell you this, Bobby Wilkerson is really ugly.

In fact, Vance County is full of ugly men.

"It must be in the water," Wilkerson said. "We've got a bunch of ugly men around here and to tell you the truth, most of them were ugly babies.

"And they had ugly daddies."

"And they've got ugly sons."

Wilkerson ought to know. He is founder and president, a well-deserved title, of the Vance County Ugly League, a homely bunch with more than 1,500 members.

In fact, if you're anybody in Vance County you have to be a member. It is status hereabouts.

"What I like to do is walk up to a stranger and say, 'Did anybody ever tell you that you're ugly? 'Cause you're about as ugly a man as I've ever seen.'

"Then I hand them a card and every one of them laughs. If you tell a man he has a big nose he might hit you, but if you tell him he's really ugly, he'll laugh, and that's the whole point, to have fun, make people laugh."

And now you know. The Vance County Ugly League is Bobby Wilkerson's way of bringing a smile to the faces of his Vance County neighbors, a way to say "How do?" and make 'em laugh.

"I just love people, I love congregating with them," Wilkerson said. "I started noticing that everybody was walking around with a long face, depressed. They'd brighten up when I'd tell 'em they were ugly and hand them a membership card.

"The world is full of problems, but I don't have any. I know how to laugh, at myself and other people.

"Last week we had the Christmas parade, so we got us a truck and put signs on it like, 'Ugly people love Christmas, too' or '1,500 and looking for more' and piled in. Everybody loved us.

"We'd yell out the back, 'Hey, lady, take the baby and put your husband up here with us. He belongs.' and they'd just laugh.

"I have never had one person get mad, ever. In fact, when I go down the street, people walk up and ask for membership cards."

There are no women in the organization, Wilkerson said, "although a bunch of them are qualified. But we don't admit people of bad character or women. Some women get mad if you call them ugly, although I don't know why, 'cause they sure are.

"And we don't take anybody with birth defects or accidents. You've got to be naturally ugly."

Because Wilkerson — a man so ugly his mama had to tie a piece of bacon around his neck to make the dog play with him — is such a professional, I asked him who in his opinion was the ugliest man around.

"That's easy," he said. "It is without a doubt Junie Grisson, the water meter man for the town, although Sen. Sam Ervin and Lt. Gov. Jimmy Green come close.

"Of course," he told me. "You're pretty ugly yourself. You may win one of these days."

As a full-fledged ugly and self-proclaimed president of the Wake County chapter, I now have a stock of membership cards and will be looking for members.

But I may not get around to you. I'll probably run out just by passing them around to the many ugly people in my office.

I mean, these folks around The News and Observer are ugly.

But I'll never reach the status of Bobby Wilkerson, the self-proclaimed "Arbiter of Ugly."

Oh well, it takes one to know one.

The Drifter

Ahoskie.

The old man walked slowly to the car.

"I 'preciate it a whole lot, Boss," he said as he crammed his padded body into the front seat. "It's mighty cold out here today. These old bones can't take it like they use'ta could."

The driver tried to be polite and not stare at the old man. He'd seen him just as he crested that last small hill, a lonely figure outlined against the mean sky with his right hand outstretched asking for a ride.

The old man rubbed his hands together in the car's warmth. He adjusted his many layers of clothes, none of them clean, and said his name was Roy.

"That's right, Boss, I travels 'most all of the time. I'm heading to Florida now. I would'a been there before now, but I had me a job up in Baltimore and I stayed too long and the cold got me.

"Don't I get tired of traveling? Naw, I reckon not. I've been doing it since the Depression, so I'm pretty much used to it by now."

He said he'd been raised on a dirt farm in west Georgia, one of eight children and when the money ran out back in the 30s, the owner told the family it had to leave.

"Some of the rest of 'em got jobs, but I always wanted to see me some of this world first, so I jumped a train one night and I ain't never been back. I guess all of them thinks I'm dead now.

"I never was one for writing letters much. To tell you the truth, Boss, I don't write so good and I figured nobody cared much what happened to me one way or the other.

"I don't mind it so bad. I can usually get me a mouthful of something to eat. Folks in churches has helped me some and the Salvation Army is real good."

The driver looked at the old man again. The acid nights of cheap wine and no food and Southern jails had done their damage. It wouldn't be long before the traveling was over.

"You want to buy me something to eat? Well that's mighty nice of you Boss and I do thank you. It's been awhile since I've had me a regular meal. But would you bring it out to me boss? Them folks might not like it if I went in and sat down."

The driver reached the crossroads where the old man had said he wanted to get out.

"We here already? Well, you take care of yourself, Boss and I want to tell you something.

"I told you it weren't so bad out here, but it is sometimes, real bad. I don't mind the cold or the not eating regular, but sometimes it does get a little bit lonesome for an old man. Some days when you's by yourself you wouldn't mind a bit if you was to die."

The old man was gone then, his image growing smaller in the rear view mirror. Then something must have gotten in the driver's eyes, because they started watering and the old man disappeared in the blur.

There I Was, Staring into the Face of Death

It is astounding how hard people will work, the discomforts they will bear, the inconvenience they will suffer, just so they can have the joys of making complete fools of themselves.

One of the standard publicity gimmicks of the Ringling Brothers and Barnum & Bailey Circus is to allow reporters to ride elephants in the elephant walk, the morning event that officially opens the circus.

What reporter could resist it? Certainly not me.

When they didn't offer me a chance to ride, I wasn't really surprised. Every place I have worked, some other reporter has gotten to ride the elephant and write the story. This year was going to be no different, it appeared.

So I begged.

David Mozes, the circus advance man, was nice. He listened as I pleaded that this must be my year. I must ride the elephant. Finally, after I threatened not to buy cotton candy for my wife and daughters, a loss in sales that could have ruined the circus industry worldwide, he consented.

Several of us media heavies — a panic-stricken Margaret Webb from WPTF radio, Maury O'Dell of the same station who spent most of the day mumbling into a walkie-talkie and WYNA's Rich McTighe in his cowboy hat — stood around, freezing our knees, noses and toes for an hour or so, waiting for our moment of glory.

Finally, after it got to snowing pretty good, here came the elephants.

Gunther Gebel-Williams, the star of the whole thing and the man in charge of the elephants, was speaking to them in rapid-fire German while a midget prodded them with a big stick. I wished both of them would stop. Elephants normally live where it is warm, and I was sure my beast was not thrilled with being in the snow while having a blond German harassing him and a midget jabbing him with a stick.

Gunther made his charges kneel, which brought my elephant's back to within six feet of the ground, and I clambered unsteadily aboard. Not too bad, I thought.

Then my beast stood up. It was like being on a giant basketball in an earthquake. The elephant went one way, and I went another.

But it would have taken a direct hit from a bazooka to dislodge me. The last thing I held that tight was my wallet at the State Fair.

From behind me I could hear Margaret Webb moaning. She was riding double with O'Dell, but it didn't help. I smiled at her. She glared at me. She didn't know I was doing my moaning on the inside.

Then we began the walk. Imagine yourself perched on the back of a drunken three-ton Brillo pad and you get the picture.

The kids loved it. They screamed and waved as we passed, not having the vaguest idea who we fools were. I waved back, not going to miss my big chance. I told them I was the mayor of Raleigh, but they didn't seem to care. Sorry about that, Mrs. Cannon.

The elephants seemed to know what was going on, and when they got to one particular place, the midget jabbed my beast and they all turned around, facing the crowd. This was so all could snap pictures at their leisure. The crowd charged, the midget kept jabbing, and Margaret Webb's elephant tried to eat my foot.

My beast would lean toward her beast, hers would lean toward mine, and elephant slobber on my boot was the result. Then our feet got tangled in a simultaneous lean and we were both temporarily crippled. My boot struck the other elephant in the eye. The elephant on the other side tried to spray dirt on me.

Finally, it was time to get off. My elephant kneeled again, and I pondered how best to dismount with hundreds of people watching. I decided on falling, so I fell.

See you next year, Webb — you chicken.

Night Stalker

Maco.

I have heard that confession is good for the soul.

I hope so, because there for awhile I felt pretty foolish.

All I wanted to do was see the famous Maco Light. I grew up hearing about the light and it has always been my favorite Tar Heel ghost story.

And now that I have a boss who will pay me real money to do silly things, I figured this was my chance.

You've heard the story, I'm sure, about how old Joe Baldwin was a conductor on the Wilmington, Manchester and Augusta Railroad that once ran through here.

One night in 1867, Joe was working on the train as it headed east to Wilmington, about 15 miles from here. Joe saw that the last car in the train had broken loose and, being the brave man he was, he leaped aboard the runaway car and tried to flag down a train coming from behind by waving his lantern.

It's a long story, but it didn't work. The train hit Joe's car, killing Joe and removing his head from his shoulders, throwing head and lantern beside the tracks.

And since then, people have been seeing strange lights along this stretch of track. Hence the famous "Maco Light."

There is something there, of that much I am sure. Too many people — and some of them were even sober — have seen it too often for it to be a hoax.

The 82nd Airborne Division has seen it. Scientists have seen it. Train engineers have stopped their trains, thinking the light that looks like a waving lantern is a real warning.

So I figured that if all of them had seen it, it would be a snap for a serious journalist like myself to catch a peek.

I am particularly interested in the light now because the tracks have been removed and I wanted to know if Joe's legend had become scrap along with the tracks.

So, armed with a camera and car doors that are easy to lock, I went in search of Joe Baldwin and the Maco Light.

Boy, is it ever dark out there at night. I got out of my car, fool that I am, and sat on my car hood looking down the track bed and waiting for a headless demon to hurt me.

Then it started raining and it got even darker. I got my umbrella out of my car and maintained my vigil standing in the pitch dark along an abandoned railroad track in the rain waiting for a ghost. It was about this time I began to feel foolish.

I never heard the man. I swear I didn't. I was standing there, getting more bored and less nervous, when I heard what sounded like, 'I'm going to cut your throat.''

Have you ever seen a grown man climb an umbrella handle?

I came unglued. I yelled and spun around, umbrella at the ready (I don't know what I was going to do with the umbrella. Perhaps I wanted to keep him dry so he could kill me comfortably) and there stood what looked like a one-eyed monster.

It really wasn't a monster. It was a very nice man with a flashlight who had seen my car parked by a dark road on a rainy night and wanted to know if I needed help.

I did, but I wasn't about to tell him what I needed. Some things are just too embarrassing.

I thanked him for his kindness and confessed that I was there looking for the light. I didn't ask his name. To do so would have required that I tell him mine and there was no way I was going to do that.

He nodded politely and walked away, leaving me standing there trying to remember how to make my heart beat again.

I didn't see Joe's light that night, but I swear I heard someone laughing quietly in the rain.

Superstar

"What we're looking for," the voice on the other end of the telephone said, "is a combination of Woody Allen, Don Knotts and Wally Cox.

"I'm told you're it."

Now how was I supposed to react to that? Woody Allen is rich and hangs around with the likes of Diane Keaton. Don Knotts is probably the funniest character actor who ever lived (when he did Barney Fife, anyway) and Wally Cox was Robert "Tony Baretta" Blake's best friend until Cox died in 1973.

Was that what he was looking for?

No, said the voice, what he had in mind was someone as ugly as Woody Allen, as skinny as Don Knotts and as wimpy as Wally Cox.

"I'm your man," I said. And the sad thing is, the voice agreed.

The voice belonged to Bill Fletcher, a fellow who makes television commercials, and he was looking for someone to help him make a commercial promoting libraries and the Governor's Conference on Libraries.

I figured this was my big chance. Bright lights. Television. Stardom. Residuals. Give my regards to Broadway.

Fat chance.

We met at the North Carolina State Library: Fletcher, who would direct our epic, cameraman Bob Sadler and producer Connie Hughes.

Considering that the commercial would be all of 30 seconds, I figured five minutes, tops, to film it.

Two hours later they were still working.

I had staggered off, exhausted.

It began with makeup. Connie, and this may shock you, made me look even weirder. By the time she finished dabbing here and there, I looked like a bookworm who hadn't seen the sun since the day they invented movable type. Resplendent in a ratty gray sweater, a narrow tie, funky old shirt and pants and bright white socks with my penny loafers, I looked like I could get arrested on general principles.

'Perfect," Fletcher announced. "You look great."

I silently swore revenge.

After diddling with the lights and camera for an awfully long time — these commercial-making folks are perfectionists — it was time for the star.

How hard could it be to put a book on a shelf, turn to my left and take out another book? It can be very hard. I did it smiling. I did it aghast. I did it shocked. I did it funny. I did it rolling my eyes like Eddie Cantor.

And then I did it again. And again.

Seven times I made that turn. Sadler and Fletcher had a conference and announced that one of those ought to be all right so we moved on to another scene. I think they gave up.

This one was easy. All I had to do was look shocked that music would be playing in a library and go "shussh."

I shushed until I was spitting sand. I shushed loud. I shushed soft. I shushed angrily. I shushed and I shushed.

I was pretty shushed out.

By the way, they really don't go "lights, camera, action" in show biz. They go, "Are you ready? All right, action," and I think they added the "action" part for me. I was so disappointed. Heck, I had even expected Fletcher to show up in riding breeches with sunglasses and a director's chair.

But it finally ended, and yes, it is very hot under those lights.

Trying to salvage something from my show-biz debut I asked Sadler, "Isn't this the way Farrah Fawcett got her start?"

He thought for a moment, too long I thought, and said gently, "No, this is the way she ended."

Goodbye, bright lights. Goodbye, stardom. Hello, typewriter.

Freedom Fighter

Fort Bragg.

It was a grand idea, at least on paper.

Bring a group of newspaper folks to Fort Bragg, let them spend 24 hours with a military unit seeing the Army from the inside and then write about it, hopefully glowing reports.

They should have known better than to invite me.

Having spent a goodly chunk of my life wearing Army green, I first suggested that rather than seeing the Army from the bottom up, a view with which I was very familiar, I check it out from the top, say hanging around with some general who had a really cushy job and learn about the modern Army over cocktails at the Officer's Club.

Lt. Dan Grigson, the public information officer in charge of me, thought that was real funny and laughed a lot while he handed me a tattered uniform.

I used to be a fairly sharp soldier, but with hair curling over my Army collar, and with knock-around boots on, I looked like a prisoner of war. It was then that I began to remember why it was I had gotten out of the Army in the first place.

I figured out that I didn't have much interest in living in the woods with the Green Berets or putting my life in the hands of a hotdog chopper pilot, so I chose to be a military policeman.

That was a lot of fun. I played cop and felt important as all get out, but then it was suppertime.

"What's that?" I foolishly asked, looking at the baseball-sized hunk of something brown the cook had put on my plate.

"We call them cannonballs," my MP friends said. "We save them so we can throw them in case of riots or war."

Not having too often cut hamburger with a knife meant I was a little out of practice, and it really did taste like you might imagine a cannonball would, but in defense of Army chow I must admit I didn't get hungry again.

In fact, for a long, long time I didn't want to think of food.

Finally, about 12:30 a.m., we got off work and headed to the barracks for the incredible joy of sleeping in a room full of other people.

It was about then I got nervous.

Here I was, lean of limb and long of hair, in a room full of semi-naked paratroopers with tattoos promising pain and destruction to all, or at least "Death Before Dishonor."

But they were really nice guys. They made me feel very welcome and even found me a bed, complete with two rough, dingy and scratchy wool blankets, but no sheets.

I did learn one important fact. All paratroopers are deaf. Or so it seems, after spending all night with a radio blaring music. The other snoring men didn't seem to mind the music, but after three hours it got a tad old.

But if you think I was about to wake up a sleeping, tattooed paratrooper cop and tell him to turn down his radio, then you've never been in the Army.

So at 3 a.m., listening to the melodious sound of the blankets scratching me raw, four snoring Killers from the Sky and Led Zeppelin, it all came back to me and once again I patted myself on the back for showing the good sense to get out of the Army. The Army and I are both better for it.

The final straw came at 5 a.m. as my eyeballs exploded when a growling sergeant turned on the lights and announced we were going to clean up the place because some colonel was coming to visit later that day.

That's when I deserted, quit, went AWOL, took a walk, bugged out and split.

So much for a day in the Army.

And now they tell me I have to return the uniform.

Marathon Man

What a nifty idea, thought I.

A mile-and-a-half run through Raleigh's Oakwood section on a nice late summer afternoon in the company of a lot of other people would have to be a lot of fun, right?

Considering that I once wanted to own an Edsel, once bet a friend real money that George McGovern would beat Richard Nixon and later bet the same friend that Jimmy Carter didn't have a chance, I should have suspected my nifty idea.

Running is the national pasttime. Everywhere you look you see people who look like they are about to die, sweating and stumbling along, all having fun.

And for reasons I do not understand, it really is fun.

It is fun putting on a pair of shorts and lacing those low-slung running shoes up tight and walking out to the street.

Then it is agony for an hour and then it is fun again when you quit and feel so proud of yourself.

Runners can be the most self-satisfied, obnoxious people you'll ever meet. We have no use for non-runners. We do not like the idea of someone coming home from work, collapsing in a favorite easy chair, lighting up a cigar and swilling down a beer while we are out there pounding our brains out.

We want everybody out there sweating and breathing hard along with us.

I started running last spring and I'm proud to say I managed to get up to almost three miles a day. Then came hot weather and since I hate sweat, I retreated to air conditioning and I Love Lucy reruns.

This seemed like a good way to start my fall running season, running with Gov. James B. Hunt Jr. and all, and how far could a mile and a half be?

It can be very far.

It all started at the corner of Bloodworth and Jones streets in Raleigh.

The governor was there, in a suspicious-looking Wolfpack red shirt and shorts (the Guv, it can be said, has cute legs).

"Bang" went the starting gun. "Rumble" went the pavement as 1,200 feet and two sets of wheelchair wheels took off. "Gasp" went my lungs. "No way, Jack" went my legs.

First I tried to keep up with the pack. Forget that. Then I tried to keep up with the knee-high blond girl. Sorry. Then I tried to keep up with a middle-aged man in long pants and wingtip shoes. I watched him disappear into a bloody haze.

Slow down, fool, I said to myself, just jog. Okay, said my body, and stopped completely.

Then I got inspired. Not far ahead of me was a guy in a wheelchair. I was desperate. Him I can beat, I thought. I know it sounds awful, but pain will do that to you. It became my driving ambition to outrun a guy in a wheelchair. It disgusted me too, but I surely did want to outrun him.

I ran like a man possessed. The guy in the wheelchair kept on rolling. Here comes a hill. I got him now. Pound those skinny legs and feet. Try not to collapse.

I almost caught the guy in the wheelchair at the top of the hill. Then we started downhill and he took off, passing people like Richard Petty at Daytona.

I stumbled on, dejected now. Only later did I learn that the guy in the wheelchair plays basketball at the Capitol City Hustlers and is one heck of an athlete.

"Hey, you're not supposed to walk, you're supposed to run," some dude with a cigar in one hand and a beer in the other yelled as I roared past.

That's when I knew I was in trouble. I thought I was running.

I guess it ended. I forget a lot of the latter parts of the run. I never caught the old guy in black wingtips. The last time I saw the little girl, she was skipping along singing. The governor was so far ahead that he'd stopped sweating when I got to the finish line.

But wait until next year. A guy in a wheelchair, indeed.

Next year I'll let the air out of his tires.

The Champ

Rose Hill.

It is the story of my life.

The one thing I have always wanted was a trophy. I didn't much care what it was for. I just wanted shiny proof that I had, in fact, taken on all comers and whipped them.

So when it was announced that the Duplin Wine Cellars in Rose Hill was going to have a grape-stomping contest. I just knew it was my chance for fame and glory.

And especially when they said the only people competing would be newspaper and television people. Most journalists are so out of shape they run out of breath snapping a pop top. And I knew they had better have oxygen tents handy for this bunch of media mighties.

I was ready for these turkeys. Pam Pope, who was in charge of this mess, told me there would be three categories: dress, stomping style and volume of juice stomped.

I figured I'd pass on dress, since true athletes like myself prefer cut-off blue jeans and T-shirt, although I did add a dashing green, plastic eye-shade, the symbol of my profession.

And there were some really big guys in the competition — such as my buddy "Hap" Hansen from WPTF radio in Raleigh — who could stomp more grapes with one stomp than I could crush by sitting down on them.

But style ... here 'I had 'em.

My theory has always been that if you can't do something well, at least be flashy.

First of all, we were given a half-bushel of muscadine grapes to stomp. Well, a foot tub full of muscadine grapes feels like a foot tub full of squishy eyeballs. It was really disgusting. Those little devils squirted around my feet and between my toes. But I did it with class.

I ran around in the tub, something none of the other media heavies even attempted. I jumped up and down to show my stamina. I hopped on one foot and then the other, showing my athletic grace.

I was beautiful. Grapes were flying everywhere. I squished juice and splashed for three long minutes. When it was over, I sat back down (after a hasty lung transplant) satisfied that I had wiped them out.

First of all, they announced that Jim Burns of WECT television in Wilmington, in a lovely red-checked sport coat, had won the dress competition. That was all right, you wear what you can afford and obviously TV folks make more dough than newspaper people.

Then they announced that Barbara Fussell, a reporter for the Rocky Mount Evening Telegram, had won the stomping style competition. (And here I think is where I became suspicious because Barbara has the same last name as the famed Duplin County family. And no, I'm not paranoid, why do you ask?)

Then came the big announcement, the champion grape stomper for 1978 was, ta da, me.

I was elated. I jumped up like the true champion I was, shook hands with my defeated and dejected fellow news persons (all of whom, by the way, deserved to lose) and grabbed my trophy.

Remember this name: Debra Joneck. Engrave it on your brain. If you meet her 20 years from now, be prepared to remind her of the day she stole my glory.

I had barely sat down and was graciously allowing the assembled photographers to take my picture and thinking of all the interviews and talk shows that would follow my championship, when Debra Joneck (remember the name) said, "There has been a mistake. The champion grape stomper is not Dennis Rogers, it is Dick Taylor from WBTV in Charlotte."

Are you kidding me? Dick Taylor? A TV dude had beaten a newspaper man? My dreams of glory faded.

But I was gracious, I must admit. I informed Taylor that he would have the trophy, but he had better be prepared to pry it from my clenched fingers after he chased me down.

But humiliation took over, and I gave up without a fight. Just natural class, I suppose. Besides, he threatened to hit me with a camera.

But there is one thing I will always remember from this episode. Debra Joneck.

I keep thinking of that old saying, "Don't get mad, get even."

And, Debra Joneck, I am a patient man.

Buckaroo

Wilson.
It was my finest hour.

I was in line at the Carolina Theater that Saturday at 11 a.m. The show had been previewed for weeks: Lash LaRue was coming to town. Hot diggity dog.

He was my favorite. His movieland competition, a fairly pudgy Whip Wilson, was a zero as far as I was concerned. Whip didn't have that snarling image I liked, he was more the clean-cut type — smiling, using his whip only to defend (choose one) the school marm, the lovable old rancher or himself.

Not Lash. I once saw Lash walk into a barroom, take a look around at the assembled ruffians and go to work. That bullwhip cracked like Jove's lightning, he snapped guns from hands the second they were drawn. He wrapped that leather around the neck of a baddie up on the balcony and pulled him down to certain doom, making him land, of course, on a table top that collapsed into splinters.

Lash was the Oakland Raiders of whip men. Mean dude. My hero.

There was the usual bill of fare that legendary day. A double feature (both Lash LaRue movies in honor of the guest) preceded by three color cartoons, a serial, a one-reel comedy and a month's worth of previews.

The box office opened at noon. By then there were several hundred of us lined up along Goldsboro Street. There were three people ahead of me. We had discussed which seats each of us wanted and had reached an understanding. I, as always, was looking for front row, left aisle.

I plunked down my nine cents admission. No one looking for that one best seat would dare come without the right change. You learn these things early in life.

I grabbed by ticket as it shot out of the slot and took off, not waiting for the ticket-taker to return my half. I bolted for the aisle, ran down that sloping concourse, gaining speed all the way. The sticky floor aided my footing as I made that hazardous turn and plopped down in my seat.

I waited patiently for the rest to arrive and in 10 minutes the theater was packed. Asking my nearest neighbor to save my seat — fistfights had been known to break out when he failed in his duty — I went back up and bought the staples, a 10-cent box of popcorn, a five-cent Pepsi and a penny Kit (chocolate, of course). Total investment, 25 cents.

No one really paid attention to the show that day, we were waiting for Lash.

He came out between the features, dressed all in black, black wrist bands, black boots, black shirt and pants (tucked into the boots), black hat, a six-shooter in a black holster on one side and a black holster for his black whip on the other.

He did a little fancy gunplay: twirling his pistol from hand to hand; flipping it in the air; over his shoulder; the fancy sideway twirl, each time the gun landing in his holster. I was impressed.

Then he took out the whip. A cheer went up. I remember two tricks clearly. The theater manager came up on stage, put a cigarette in his mouth and stood on one side of the stage. Lash stood on the other.

The whip snaked through the air, back over his shoulder, and then shot forward like a living thing, nipping that cigarette out of the man's mouth from what looked like 30 feet away.

Then Lash turned to the mob and said those famous words, "I need a volunteer from the audience."

Every hand went up, including mine. He took forever, looking across the horde. Finally, he looked down at the front row. He scanned the row and the eyes that had frightened hundreds of desperados landed on me. He pointed and said to come on up.

I must have walked up to the stage. I remember floating, however.

He handed me a piece of paper with his picture on it, about the size of a dollar bill.

I stood on one side of the stage, held the picture with both hands at arm's length in front of me, facing Lash.

I was scared to death.

"Now don't move," he said. Move? I was paralyzed. I could hardly breathe I was so excited.

The whip came from nowhere. I saw his arm move and something flicked in front of my eyes and the paper split in two.

The cheers ring in my ears to this day.

Greater glory hath no sidewalk cowboy. On that day I was the envy of every buckaroo on the block.

You should have seen me swagger back to my seat.

Rock and Roll Never Forgets

I feel sorry for this younger generation.

Those of us who grew up in the '50s had something that helped us transcend those difficult years twixt twelve and thirty-five, something that made the zits tolerable, something to hold on to in a troubled time.

We had rock 'n' roll.

But rock 'n' roll is in trouble now, challenged by a new beat, this one with lighted dance floors, stacked heels and something called The Hustle.

It is the Day of the Disco. Darn it.

But not everyone is a Disco Dude or Dudette. Some are, in fact, worried about this turn of the turntable.

With abject apologies to the New York Sun, edition of September 27, 1897, I offer the following in the hope it will not only hasten the death of disco, but will give solace to the few of us who still love real rock 'n' roll:

"Dear Columnist: I am eight years old.

"Some of my little friends say there is no rock 'n' roll.

"Papa says, 'If you read it in the N&O, it's so.'

"Please tell me the truth, is there rock 'n' roll?

"Signed, Twinkle MacFarland, East Overshoe."

Twinkle, your little friends are wrong. They have been affected by the double-knit of a polyester age. They do not believe except they boogie. They think that nothing can be which is not danceable by their little feet.

Yes, Twinkle, there is rock 'n' roll. It exists as certainly as Chuck Berry and the Rolling Stones exist, and you know that they kick out of the jams to give your life its highest beauty and joy.

Alas! How dreary would be the world if there were no rock 'n' roll. It would be as dreary as if there were no blue jeans. There would be no T-shirts, no halter tops, no long hair, no music to make tolerable this existence.

Not believe in rock 'n' roll? You might as well not believe in Buddy Holly. You might get your papa to hire men to watch in all the record shops on allowance day to catch Rod Stewart, but even if they did not see him strutting in, what would that prove?

Nobody sees rock 'n' roll. The most real things in the world are those that neither disco freaks nor John Travolta fans can see.

Did you ever see Mick Jagger singing inside your stereo? Of course not, but that's no proof he is not there. Nobody can conceive or imagine all the rockers that are unseen and unseeable in the world.

You can buy an album and see what makes the music inside, but there is still a veil covering the unseen world which not even the richest disco dude, with a three-piece white suit, an open collar and gold jewelry, can tear apart.

Only faith, concert tickets, a loathing for disco music, a volume knob set on high and rocking around the clock can push aside that curtain so you can view and picture the supernatural beauty and glory that is rock 'n' roll.

Is it all real? Ah, Twinkle, in all the world there is nothing else real and rocking.

No rock 'n' roll? Bless Chuck Berry. He lives and lives forever. A thousand years from now, Twinkle, nay ten times ten thousand years from now he will continue to make loud the rooms of childhood.

Those Empty Blue Suede Shoes

January 8, 1979.

Had Elvis lived, few people would have noticed that today would have been his 44th birthday.

I, for instance, would not have written this column. His birthday would have been a non-event, celebrated only by his friends and a few superfans who do that sort of thing.

And, most certainly, Gov. James B. Hunt Jr. would not have signed an official state proclamation marking the event.

But Elvis did not live. He crumpled to the floor of his Memphis mansion, a tired, sick, middle-aged, overweight man, dying alone on his bathroom floor.

I was not an Elvis fan. I was, however, a fan of a greasy redneck from Tupelo, Miss., by way of Memphis. That redneck could barely play a guitar, but he could rip out Big Mama Thornton's screaming blues like he invented them.

I loved "Jailhouse Rock" and "Hound Dog" and, probably the greatest blues song of my generation, that moving, picture postcard misery, "Heartbreak Hotel."

I did not love the Las Vegas glitter that became Elvis.

Elvis was more than a singer of songs and a seller of records, in spite of all Tom Parker could do, when he blew into the nation's radios more than two decades ago. For instance, he was the first to make hair a political and social issue.

We wore burr-headed flat tops. He wore greasy ducktails.

Lest we forget, Fonzie did not invent the juvenile delinquent image so much associated with the 50s. John Travolta did not invent the ducktail haircut.

It was Elvis Aaron Presley who sent us to our mirrors, Wildroot Creme Oil in one hand and a comb in the other. Most men did not know how to use two mirrors, but we knew. We knew a properly built ducktail was a work of art and an artist looks at his work from all sides.

Slap on the Wildroot, comb it back on the sides (carefully preserving the comb tracks), curl it down in front. Reach back to where the side waves meet and, either with a comb or fingertips, crease it down the middle.

The core of what he taught us was simple but earthshaking: Adults don't always know best.

Adults decided everything, the music we heard, the clothes we wore, the way we cut our hair, our slang.

But Elvis, who was uniformly despised by adults, gave us what it took to change all that. He made adults start paying attention to us, whether they wanted to or not. No longer did we want to be small adults. We wanted to be what we were. It was all right to be a teen-ager. The country became youth-oriented.

But as the world changed (some would disagree whether it changed for the better or the worse), so did Elvis.

He was a terrible actor in rotten movies, but at least he didn't pretend they were anything but what they were, fluffs for the faithful.

The music withered. The edge was gone, the humor, the anger. It was packaged pop in sequins and a man whose job it was to hand Elvis scarves so he could bless them with holy sweat and throw them to the multitudes.

And the women who fought for them in the late sixties had clucked disapprovingly at young girls who went beserk over the Beatles five years earlier.

At the end of it all we had another Elvis, one who neither looked nor sounded like the original; a money-making clone. And when he died he became the biggest money maker of all.

I have a friend named Ailene and we often discuss the Elvis Phenomenon. She is a true believer. She had cried at Graceland.

I mentioned to her that I thought much of the Elvis memorabilia was tacky, morbid and tasteless. I do not need a clock in Elvis' stomach to remember him.

"Some of it is," she said, "But I've bought a lot of it.

"Don't you understand — that's all we've got left now."

So listen to all-Elvis radio stations today, count the number of North Carolina license plates bearing his name (10), gaze at the plaster bust of him that plays "Don't Be Cruel" when you push the button in the back.

I'll remember that other guy.

Git Down, Boogie Man

Gold Rock.

"You bump?" she asked.

"Do what?" I replied.

"You bump?" she asked again.

"Ah ... well ... not on purpose," I replied.

"No, I mean do you do the bump, you know, the dance?" she asked, beginning to back away from me.

"Oh ... no," I said as she disappeared. I did not feel like Humphrey Bogart at that moment.

That's the way it went when your fearless correspondent took two dollars in hand, screwed his courage up tight and went off to the world of the disco.

Having seen "Saturday Night Fever," I figured I was ready, and when I heard the music from down a long hall and through two doors, I knew the time had come to check out the disco scene.

Relax. All a disco is is Top 40 radio without weather reports. There are plenty of commercials, such as, "Hey out there, you're getting it on at the Disco City Lounge. We do it here every Tuesday, Wednesday, Friday and Saturday night. Hey, here's a special request. Let's get down."

"Getting down," pronounced "Gittin' downnnnn" and, alternately, "Getting it on," pronounced "Git it ooonnnnn" is apparently why you go to a disco. How one is to know when one has it either "down" or "on," I couldn't say. You must just know that sort of thing when it happens to you, sort of like being in love.

The usual disco is spearheaded by a person called a "disco jock," as opposed to the radio "disc jockey." The only difference is that a jockey tells you what time it is while a jock tells you to "get it on" a lot.

The jock stands, or sometimes sits, at one end of the room with two turntables and a stack of records.

The music is not rock 'n' roll. It is disco music, which means horns have replaced guitars and the beat is everything. The only recognizable words I caught were "shake your booty" and "Play that funky music, white boy."

The music you hear, for the most part, isn't the same that radio stations use to fill time between commericals and weather reports. Instead, the disco music-makers get their popularity — and their bucks — because people like to get it "on" and "down" in discos.

And the volume is very important. There must a lot of it. If you can't feel it in your chest, it ain't loud enough.

The people who go to discos are very nice people, and the Disco City Lounge here just north of Rocky Mount at Interstate 95 is a very nice lounge. There are a lot of buttons left unbuttoned and hair spray sprayed. And that's on the men.

Basically, it is what we old folks used to call a "record hop." There are boys at some tables and girls at others and a dude playing records — "spinning platters" it used to be called — and occasionally the twain meet. The boys usually ask the girls to dance, but as proved by the lovely lass who asked me about bumping, sometimes even dolts such as I luck out.

They dance together and sit apart for awhile, then they dance and sit together. I guess that's when they get it "on."

Or is it "down."

I never can keep those straight.

Band on the Run

Wrightsville Beach.

It scares you the first time it happens.

You wake up in a motel room, curtains drawn, the first light of day sneaking through a crack in the curtains.

You wonder where you are, what place is this?

Such is life for a band on the run.

The North Carolina Symphony is a band on the run, from one side of the state to the other and back again, 73 musicians strong, 250-plus concerts each season, close to 20,000 miles by bus, breathing diesel fumes, playing cards and knitting, 40 weeks in a row and no pay for the other 12, playing music for a quarter of a million people a year.

It is late Monday afternoon, a morning concert for school children already played, an evening concert awaiting. Before this week ends, the orchestra will travel and play in Fayettevlle, High Point and Asheville and then back to Raleigh again, more than 750 miles on a bumpy bus, trying to kill the hours and save the spirit.

The evening's concert is in Kenan Auditorium on the campus of the University of North Carolina at Wilmington, a splendid building with a curving porch, spacious lobby and stately columns. All the musicians will see are cramped backstage space, a stage floor covered with snaking black cables and lights in their eyes. They could be anywhere.

The members of the orchestra, in look-alike black and white tuxedos for the men and black dresses for the women, like mourners at a state funeral, drift to the buses at 7 p.m. — an hour before the baton is due to fall.

There are two buses, one called the Animal Bus, the other the Corpse Bus. I choose to ride the Animal Bus.

I step in, stumble over a can and walk across a floor strewn with cigarette butts, scraps of paper and litter bags filled with more cans.

Two card games are under way before the bus leaves the parking lot. The players never look up as the driver wades through traffic to the campus.

It is 7:40 when we arrive and the musicians hurry to the stage door, drop off their coats and head for their chairs on the stage, never looking out at the hundred or so who have come early.

It is a raucous sound that fills the building, instruments and their players being tuned and warmed up, last cigarettes hurriedly smoked outside the door, music placed on stands, chairs banging and feet shuffling.

Suddenly it grows quiet. Concert master Paul Gorski looks at oboist Ronald Weddle and, as is the tradition in orchestras, asks for an "A." The oldest of all instruments sounds the note and everyone makes last-minute tunings to the eerie sound.

At precisely 8 p.m., Conductor John Gosling leaves his dressing room and strides to stage right where he stands for a moment and then walks onstage to applause. He speaks for a few moments about the evening's program, then turns, looks at the talent assembled before him and lowers the baton. Music fills the hall.

No one thinks of card games or long nights in lonely rooms or the miles left to drive this week. Every musician there is part of the music that is being made, moving as one instrument, flowing together through the music of Ives, Haydn, Saint-Saens and Paganini, from discordant to lush.

A break comes in the program and several musicians stand outside. They won't be needed for the next selection.

They talk, warily at first, but warming as the night wears on, of the other side of the orchestra, the motels that won't take them anymore because of wild parties, tales that elicit more giggles than facts, the time a famous soloist spent all night playing poker and ended up at the airport the next morning, broke and still in his formal white tie and tails for the plane ride home, complaints about a schedule that takes them from the middle of the state to the coast to the mountains and back to the middle of the state again, all in one week, of weirdos they have known and loved.

It is over in two short hours, a magnificent evening of music from a magnificent collection of musicians, and everyone rushes back to the buses.

There is more night to go. Some will spend it at a free beer bash, some will spend it watching the finals of the NCAA basketball tournament, some will retire early to read, write letters or sleep; for every card player there is a knitter, for every beer drinker a bridge fanatic, whatever helps make it through the week.

The weekend is a long way away.

When the Piano Man Played the Blues

Maysville.

The whispery blues come softly from the tape player: Duke Ellington's "C-Jam Blues" it's called. The piano man hums along with his recorded music.

He pulls out a handkerchief, excuses himself in a quiet voice and dabs at tears that form in the corners of his aging eyes.

"I can't help it, I just cry when I hear something that pretty," the piano man says. "When I play I'm in another world. I don't hear nothing but the music."

His name is Williard M. "Bill" Wooten, the hep cat grown old, 40 years or so of playing jazz and blues behind him now.

"We were real gone in those days," he said. The music plays on. It brings up images of slinky ladies on a chic Saturday night in Harlem when the Cotton Club was the center of the universe for the jazzmen.

"Oh yeah. I played at the Cotton Club." He smiles. "I was there the night Ella Fitzgerald came in. That was some kind of a place."

Bill Wooten was born to jazz 66 years ago.

"My daddy was awful, a terrible musician," Wooten said, using that reverse praise found only in music, where "awful" means good and "terrible" is high praise indeed. "He played the mandolin, trumpet and violin. He trained all us kids."

After high school he and a friend hitchhiked to Tennessee where Wooten made his music, sang in the choir and played football.

After college came more football, with the professional Black Panthers of Knoxville.

But it was soon back to music.

"We'd play some of them Saturday night fish fries," he said. "A fellow would get him a house and a band and he'd run an open bar, sell you anything you wanted, booze or drugs, and the police never bothered us. I can tell you a dozen people that were killed at those things, but no one was ever arrested.

"We played in some rough places. Many times I've had to get behind the piano for safety."

"We'd play out on the street at the Southern Club in Greensboro, playing for tips. We'd go to Market Street and buy us a pig foot and a bowl of beans. That's what we lived on."

But it was hard to make a living being a jazzman in North Carolina, so Wooten became a full-time high school bandleader, saving his jazz for weekend nights.

He brought life to his high school bands, he said, introducing to Dunn that famous quick-step march that used to be the symbol of black high school bands.

"We'd stop the parade everywhere we went," he remembers. "Those other bands would walk by like they were dead and we'd come in a-jiving. The crowds loved us."

Meanwhile, the jazzman was still working.

"I used to go play at the Guys and Dolls Club in Fayetteville, playing for the strippers," he said. "We'd play from 9 p.m. to 4 a.m. and then I'd go back to Dunn and teach all day.

"Our kind of music started to die when jukeboxes came in," Wooten said. "They used to hire a band but then they could get a jukebox for next to nothing and they didn't hire us anymore.

"I still get a few gigs. I play at music stores sometimes, at some private parties, but I never get any black gigs. They want that jukebox music. It makes my heart bleed.

"You get addicted to music, all you want to do is sit down and play.

"When I play, I'm playing one chorus and thinking about the next one, thinking what I could do to make it different. You don't see nobody, all you're looking for is that lost chord, the special one to make the music better.

"Sometimes I'd be up there playing and somebody would yell, 'Blow that box, man, blow that box.' I love it.

"I may be 66 and crippled with arthritis, but there ain't nothing wrong with my hands.

"All I need is a piano and I can play all night."

"C-Jam Blues" comes around on the tape again. We sit quietly, listening to the smooth sounds of Bill Wooten at the electric piano.

His eyes leave the room, remembering what it was like when the piano man played the blues.

Blow that box, piano man, blow it one more time.

The Queen of Country Music

It is a hot, crowded and noisy place, a long way from the excitement you might imagine.

Cigarette smoke hangs in a blue sheet in the humid September air. Spilled drinks make the floor feel tacky.

The lady stands behind a tattered gold drape, twitching slender fingers on which eight diamond and silver rings fit heavily.

At her side is Big Jim Webb, a scowling man with a pompadour who seems to like no one but the lady.

A hush falls over the place as she bounces nervously. Then comes the big voice from nowhere.

"Ladies and gentlemen, Loretta Lynn."

She started smiling when the voice started talking. Now, smile firmly in place, she bounds onto the stage to be met by a solid wall of noise. The crowd, sweltering on the Sunday afternoon, stops fanning and starts clapping. Flashbulbs explode into tiny pinpoints of light in the big room, winking love at the lady they had come to see.

For the next hour she sang to them, songs that until then had been only grooves in plastic.

Dressed in a floor-length, flowered cocktail dress, she looks like a 43-year-old millionaire (which she is) entertaining at a country club. She doesn't pander to the audience with spangles and cowgirl suits. She doesn't have to.

"I'm not the 'Queen'," she would tell me later. "I'm just who I am. I'm just me."

I had come to Dorton Arena on the state fairgrounds to see what it was like backstage at a Loretta Lynn concert.

It begins with chicken.

When Loretta plays Raleigh, the faithful from all over bring food. It is spread in a dingy, lower-level dressing room well in advance. Hungry crew and band members, groupies, policemen and privileged fans crowd in for the home-cooked goodies.

But not Loretta. She waits in the bus, a rolling home parked within spitting distance of the stage door. Friends come and go, but Loretta can't. She is rich, talented, famous and a prisoner of it all.

Moments before her entrance, after her band has warmed up the crowd with six songs, there is a flurry at the door. Big Jim appears first, watching everything and trusting no one. He quickly leads Loretta through the small crowd and up onto the security of the stage.

The show is sedate. No one screams. They listen, applaud at the right times, then wait for more. When she finishes 55 minutes later, she dances off to respectable applause. The lust-inspired frenzy of other shows can be let loose. It is time for the second half of the show: Conway Twitty.

Loretta signs autographs for a few moments and then Big Jim takes her back to the bus to change and await the finale, a duet with Twitty. The friends and crewmen come and go again from the bus, but not Loretta. She sits and waits.

After the show, she signs autographs for 45 minutes in the grueling heat. She returns to the bus only when the very last fan has pressed toward her an album or picture (conveniently on sale at the foot of the stage).

Now Big Jim, reluctantly, it seems, lets me on the bus to meet the lady.

We sit in hushed comfort. An air conditioner, insulation and heavy curtains block out the crowd and noise. We could be anywhere in the world, day or night, and I wouldn't know. Neither would she.

She talks to Bill Morrison, the N&O critic, and I watch her. Dressed in fancy jeans, a T-shirt advertising her dude ranch and silver high heels left over from the cocktail dress, she speaks in that flat, twangy Kentucky drawl that is her trademark.

I ask her one question: Where does it come from, this incredible energy to travel constantly, sing day after day, live cooped up in a bus and then spend 45 minutes signing autographs before the long, overnight drive back to Nashville?

"I wouldn't be worthy of being brought back to sing if I was too good to sign autographs," she says. "They have been real good to me out there."

Out there, Rufus Edmisten, North Carolina's attorney general, has blown his political cool. He sang one song with Loretta, and he is still bubbling an hour later.

"I served subpoenas on Richard Nixon, and I have spoken everywhere, but I swear, this is the most exciting thing in my life," he says, still there long after the show and crowd are gone.

It is getting dark. The concert ended 90 minutes ago, and now Big Jim is driving the bus out of the parking lot.

Behind, in the gathering gloom, stand 22 people. They

waited until the last, hoping Loretta would leave the bus again, just one more time.

She didn't.

Stargazer

Kinston.

Her name is Shelia Brinson and these are the dreams of a country girl:

"I used to sing in church every Sunday and I loved it. I'd watch all those late-night television shows and listen to the radio and just know I could sing as good as they could.

"About two years ago we got us a little four-piece band called 'Scotch and Soda' — my nickname is Scotch, you know, I gave it to myself — and we played civic clubs and high schools, mostly for free.

"I got called for this audition with a country show, and they put me on the first time at the fire department in Saratoga. I saw that poster with my name on it, and I was so proud.

"I stood backstage that night and I was really excited. This was the dream, and I walked out there in that tight, white jumpsuit with the green sequins that my Mama made.

"I thought to myself, 'Either you've got it or you don't,' but I was scared to death. After I got out there I relaxed and got a real thrill when the crowd smiled back at me.

"I felt up, proud, happy, like I was going to bust.

"That night I went home and dreamed it all over again. When I woke up the next morning I knew music was something I never wanted to give up. The real world was so dull.

"I've had a lot of offers since then. Some guys think I'm pretty and sexy and they'll say 'I'm going to make you big,' or do this or do that for me, if I'll travel with them and be their mistress.

"It breaks your heart when they try to hustle you like that. They're not serious about what you're the most serious about in the whole world.

"I get discouraged, but if I've got to be something I'm not (in order) to become something I want to be, I'll just be what I am, where I am.

"Some of those guys feel like singers are a dime a dozen, and I guess a lot of girls did sleep their way to Nashville like they say, and no one would know about it if I did but me — but that's one too many.

"All I want to do is sing. Is that too much to ask for?

"I've always strived to be different. I'll admit it, I like for people to notice me. I drive a customized Corvette, and I won't go out of the house unless my makeup is just right, my hair is in place and my jeans are pressed. I want them to see me the same way they see me on stage. I want to look like a star, all the time.

"I'm a big show-off, and if I've got a crowd, I want to impress them. I want them to remember me. I want people around me to say, 'Hey, I knew Scotch back then ...'

"I guess you have to be patient to get something you want so bad as I want to sing. But it hurts to wait for a break. It's miserable to want something so bad.

"I want to run out in the middle of the street and holler, 'Help me somebody, give me some direction, help me make it to the top.'

"But all I get are promises, the wrong kind.

"I even thought about pouring soap flakes in the fountain and then singing while it bubbled, just to get people to hear me and pay me some attention.

I may have to give up being a singer and stay in Kinston, but I won't ever give up the dream.

"No, sir, I'll always dream

"You don't have to have help to dream."

Sunshine and Shadows

It was 5:30 a.m. Sunday, the sky frozen black, the air so clear and clean that the stars didn't twinkle. They stared down unblinking and unfriendly.

Nothing moved at that hour. Traffic lights played out their three-color light show to no audience. The hum of the signal boxes carried for a hundred yards in the stillness.

There was no one on Fayetteville Street Mall. No buses chugged downtown. A solitary car sat in a government parking lot.

Lights burned at the bus station, comforting travelers who slumped in fatigue and boredom. A taxi engine rumbled in the darkness, hidden in the shadows with only a steamy fog to mark its place.

The squirrels and the pigeons slept on the Capitol grounds.

The cowboy and the lady were hungry, ravenous after an all-night party they had hosted. It had been a delightful affair, the last guest had just left moments before and now the couple, she in chic black and silky white, he in fashionable boots and jeans, were in search of food at that loneliest of hours.

The city asleep had many faces. Residential neighborhoods slumbered gently, here a porch light left on by mistake, there a bathroom light on early. Somewhere, maybe miles away, a dog barked once.

But the downtown city streets don't sleep so soundly.

Not everyone has a home and not everyone who has one wants to be there.

Suddenly, rounding an almost forgotten corner, the cowboy and the lady found bright lights, a restaurant in the frozen night.

It was a service station one time, now it was a sanctuary.

The cowboy and the lady entered the restaurant, a warm, brightly lit place where time doesn't matter, where clocks have no hands and Willie sings on the juke box.

They were not alone.

Sitting at the counter was a policeman. It was hard to tell from the way he rubbed his bleary face if he was coming to work or going home. His face was tired, but was it tired from the boredom and misery he had seen or was about to see?

He sat and watched his steaming cup of coffee, stripped off his official veneer of tough, efficient crimefighter. He was in the sanctuary and he could be what he really was — tired, not very happy, alone. But he kept his back to the wall, his face to the door.

A bag lady sat by herself in a booth, her shopping bag crammed full at her feet. But she was not alone. She mumbled to an imaginary friend and breakfast guest, humming a snatch of a song, speaking parts of words, head always moving, giving her shopping bag a reassuring touch with her left foot from time to time.

She looked up at the clock, not that she had anywhere to go, rather gauging how long they would let her sit here where it was warm and safe, away from the chilly demons who stalked her darkened streets and dreams.

Through the steamed-over plate glass, two headlights flashed on the windows, the steam spreading the light until the whole window was aglow.

Four faces glanced toward the door. The policeman stopped his cup halfway between counter and lips, glancing up without moving. His body was tired, his mind numb, but his reflexes were working.

The bag lady turned with a start, fright flashing through her eyes, her left hand automatically reaching for the bag at her feet, ready to flee if necessary and hoping it wouldn't be.

The cowboy looked up, casually wondering who next would join the pre-sunrise meal.

The fancy lady turned and looked over her shoulder. Was it someone from the party? Could the good times go on? Maybe the party wasn't really over.

There were three people in the doorway, a young man and two women. The cowboy nodded to himself. He had seen trios like that before, a hustler and his women, he figured.

The lady didn't notice, she didn't know them and the country ham in front of her was more important.

The cop looked the longest but then he too forgot them and went back to his coffee and private dread.

The bag lady hummed a forgotten tune; she felt safe again.

Willie Nelson sang "Whisky river take my mind ..."

A promise of dawn lit the eastern sky. The cowboy and the lady smiled at each other and went home. As they left, the cop stirred off his stool and the bag lady didn't leave a tip.

The night was over.

No one needs a sanctuary in the light.

Wilmington.

The moist night air hangs heavy in this old city.

The mingled smells of swamp water, concrete, people and industry blend in the superheated air that is still not cool, though the hottest day of the year is mercifully ending.

The air muffles sound, like an out-of-focus picture softens the edge of reality, adding a sense of beauty and wonder to the commonplace.

The sounds in the parking lot are happy ones. The muffled whump of car doors slamming. The slurred chuckle from two old friends. The tinkle of laughter as the women arrive almost always in twos, never alone and rarely, if ever, in quartets.

This is Ladies Night at the hotel bar, a place where men and women share music, booze, cigarettes and dreams.

For four hours they will fight the demon together, that uncaring, shapeless fear that lives in their stomachs like a stone.

Its name is loneliness and it can do cruel things.

"I'm here just about every Wednesday night," the secretary named Judy shouts above the whirling din that is rising inside. "That's the night the salesmen are in town.

"The girls here are from Wilmington and the men are always from Raleigh or Charlotte, it seems like."

Fantasy, not fact, is the rule here. Last names are hard to come by this early in the evening. No one wants to know too much, too soon. No one asks about wives or husbands or children yet.

That comes later, after the booze has loosened the noose of inhibition that is the sidekick of loneliness. Then decisions about tonight or other nights, phone numbers or one last drink will be made. Not now, not while there are still choices.

There are many women in the room, but even more men. They are not kids. They are in their 30s mostly, a few younger and many older.

They come here with their eyes open, knowing how to play the game without getting hurt too often or too deeply. Women rarely refuse to dance and men always ask several different women to dance at least early in the evening.

Later on, around 11, partnerships are made. Two people feel right dancing together. Maybe she is tall and so is he. Maybe neither of them is handsome, and they both know it.

The tables get pushed together, the chairs slid closer, the heads lean toward each other and now he is buying the drinks.

The talk is of safe things. What do you do? That sounds interesting. Where are you from? Oh, then do you know ...

Out in the hallway, between the woman who stamps hands with glow-in-the-dark ink and the men's room, a fight breaks out.

One man hits another in the mouth. And then they embrace, both apologizing. The sea of people flowing to the restrooms during the intermission engulfs them again, the incident little more than something to talk about until the band comes on and makes talk useless.

They start leaving by 1 a.m. Secretaries have to get up

early, Judy says. She has been yawning since midnight.

A married salesman named Gary, who has been dancing with Judy's friend Debbie, looks at his watch and back at the women as they rise to leave.

Debbie never looks back as she walks out of the door into the still-hot air.

Gary turns slowly away from the door, takes a last gulp of 80-cent beer and shrugs.

"She wasn't that hot anyway," he says.

Ladies Night has ended and out in the parking lot no one laughs anymore.

Kinston.

It was the ultimate putdown of modern youth.

"The youngun's are too sorry today to even chase a foul ball," one old man told another as they watched the baseball disappear into the humid night, sinking rapidly behind the fence.

It was all I could do to keep from chasing it myself.

For a skinny kid who grew up shagging fouls beyond the fences at Fleming Stadium where the mighty Wilson Tobs held forth on summer nights, the sight of a foul ball is enough to make even tired feet move.

Baseball is a comforting sport. It doesn't change. No matter where the stadium or the name of the team, a stranger can walk into a ballpark and feel at home.

The Kinston Eagles were flying high. It was the beginning of the second half of the Carolina League season and their record was 4-1. Their opponents, the Winston-Salem Red Sox, were in town for a few days and things were going well.

The night air was so hot and humid you could see it.

"You'd better buy a program before you faint," the sweating vendor with the roaring voice announced.

"These are all-purpose Eagles souvenir programs. You can read 'em, sit on 'em or fan with 'em. Get 'em now before you faint."

He was doing a brisk business, but he was not so busy

that he couldn't keep up with the action.

A sizzler was slapped toward first base, but the young man moved a split second too late and bobbled the ball.

"I'd better not see that again," the vendor roared in a voice that rattled windows blocks away. Even the players smiled.

It was a typical ballpark crowd, old men who wouldn't think of missing a home game, young families just being together, young boys with a pocketful of change and lights in their eyes.

They were unmercifully cruel to the opposing players, solidly biased in favor of the home team and sure that the umpires were in the pay of the Devil himself.

In other words, they were just like fans in any sport anywhere. They had come for a good time.

Mel Barrow, an Eagle outfielder, gave the fans their first chance to really get into the action.

Barrow, a crowd pleaser, hit a single and then tried to steal second. It appeared to me that he was out, but the umpire called him safe. The crowd roared its approval.

Then Barrow, perhaps made cocky by his good fortune or the crowd electricity, tried to steal third. This time he appeared to be safe, but the ump called him out.

The ump giveth and the ump taketh away.

The crowd erupted. The umpire who made both calls was compared unfavorably to all manner of evil. Barrow jumped up and down and argued. Manager Leo Mazzone came from the dugout for a few choice words with the ump, but his heart wasn't in it. He knew Barrow was out, but the crowd was having none of it.

Barrow muttered a little too loudly on his way to the dugout, prompting a short — but firm — reply from the ump, accompanied by a flip of the thumb in the ageless signal that said in hand motion what the ump told the Eagle player: "Mel, get out of here."

The crowd yelled even more bloodthirsty threats and an off-duty policeman edged into the stands, just in case.

Barrow played it for all it was worth, taking forever to pick up his glove and leave the ballpark, the yells of the crowd ringing in his ears. The ump waited him out, listening to the taunts all the time.

Two plays later, the crowd had already forgotten the incident and was back in the game.

You could see summer lightning over the centerfield fence as a thunderstorm moved in. With each shimmering flash of light, the heads of kids peeking over the centerfield fence were sharply outlined.

It was a comforting sight, somehow. As long as summertime kids will go out to a ballgame and sneak a peek over the fence, in hopes of seeing a game or getting a homerun ball, can things really be all that bad?

Wendell.

She passed this way briefly.

At 19 she had little time to make her mark upon the world, but no one at Peace College in Raleigh, or in the little Wake County town of Wendell, will ever be able to look at yellow roses without thinking of Jackie Lee Ammons.

And when the 193 young women graduates of Peace College, class of 1979, received their diplomas in a bittersweet ceremony, they paused for a moment to remember Jackie, a campus leader, a friend, who died a week before graduation.

Jackie's friends still remembered how she looked three weeks before that night of the spring dance on April 20, her last night among them.

"She wore a peach dress and she looked so good with her dark tan, it was the prettiest I had ever seen her," Janet Bender of Pollocksville remembers. "I had never seen her happier. She danced the last dance of the evening, a song called 'The Last Dance,' with her brother, and they really cut loose. We all had a great time."

After the dance about 2 a.m., Jackie, her brother Fred and two friends left Raleigh for a weekend on Topsail Island, where Jackie's parents, Mr. and Mrs. William J. Ammons, were waiting.

Suddenly, at the intersection of N.C. 11 and N.C. 111, between Kinston and Pink Hill — a dangerous intersection at which Jackie herself had almost had an accident shortly before the beach trip — the car missed a turn. Jackie was slammed forward, her head smashing into the dash.

She was taken to Duplin General Hospital in Kenansville then transferred immediately to a hospital in Wilmington. There the wait began.

Her family gathered at her bedside as she lay unconscious. They spent much of their time in a borrowed camper in the parking lot. The word spread quickly across the Peace College campus and around her hometown of Wendell: Jackie was badly hurt.

Dozens of college students headed for Wilmington to be at her side, joining the family, Peace President S. David Frazier, faculty members, staff members, two deans and dozens of friends from Wendell. They brought food, kind words and love.

"We went down there to do what we could, to console the family, but the Ammons family ended up consoling us, taking care of us," Laurie Sikes remembered. "People who had gone to Peace, or whose daughters had gone to Peace, opened their homes in Wilmington to us to give us somewhere to stay."

Back in Wendell, on the Ammons family farm, it was tobacco planting time. Without being asked, almost 100 friends and neighbors gathered at the Ammons home.

For two days they planted the tobacco, cleaned the Ammons home and trimmed the lawn — country people doing what country people have always done when there was tragedy in their community, taking care of their own.

Jackie had carved out her niche during her two years on the Peace campus. For the last two semesters she had been a straight-A student, elected to Phi Theta Kappa honor society.

She was a scholarship basketball player and tri-captain of the Green Giants, president of the Fellowship of Christian Athletes, selected to an All-Tournament volleyball team, selected by the Peace faculty for "Who's Who in American Junior Colleges" and chosen by fellow students as one of the eight most outstanding students in her class.

The Dean's List, published after her death, carries her name. Her basketball jersey, numbered 44, was retired in her honor.

After a week, Jackie's body began to fail. Her vital signs began to worsen, her temperature fell, there was evidence of serious brain damage. All the years spent working on her family farm, all the years playing basketball and volleyball had made her healthy and strong.

Perhaps it was her strength that kept her going so long — her strength and the yellow roses.

Each day, while Jackie lay dying, her father brought a yellow rose to her bedside and pressed it into her hand. Yellow was her color. You could always spot those bright yellow gym shorts and the bright yellow sweat shirt on campus.

After 16 days, Jackie Lee Ammons died quietly, at 4 a.m. on May 6. Her family and friends were at her side.

More than 1,500 people gathered in the Wendell Baptist Church when Jackie Lee Ammons was buried. Every inch of the building was crammed — the sanctuary, the vestibule and all the classrooms. Still, half of the crowd could not even get inside the building.

The church was filled with yellow roses.

"She was as lovable a person as ever passed through Peace Collge," Frazier said, holding a small plastic model of Mickey Mouse, a gift from Jackie's spring trip to Walt Disney World. "She was always doing some little thoughtful deed to brighten other people. We had even discussed her coming back here to join our faculty. She was exactly the kind of person you'd want to have working with young people as a coach and teacher."

For most people, Jackie Lee Ammons was a college kid killed in a senseless accident. But for the young women of Peace College, for the people of Wendell, for the Ammons family, she will live in every yellow rose they see.

The race begins in the traditional way. The athletes lining up at the starting line. The starter raising his pistol, firing one shot and off they go.

The young man jumped into the lead immediately, running with ease, fluid grace as he shot into the front of the 440-yard race. He ran effortlessly. The race was never in doubt.

Behind him, running with more difficulty, were three younger runners, struggling along at that distance, more huffing and puffing than speed, but on they came, their eyes never leaving the track in front of them.

They finished in respectable time, and they were all met by the hugs and honors that go to athletes who complete a grueling race.

But who is that still on the track? The race was over, everyone thought. Who is that still running?

His name is Jeffrey.

Jeffrey was only about one-quarter of the way around the track when the winner flashed across the finish line, barely halfway around when the other three crossed the stripe.

Then he was all alone, running not for glory, but for pride.

Jeffrey ran as hard as he could, stumbling, agonizing with every step, uncoordinated, halting, barely keeping his feet straight, but on he came.

The crowd spotted Jeffrey coming into the final turn, just over 100 yards from the finish. The applause began then.

The applause grew as Jeffrey chugged his way down the home stretch, a grin across his face, his cheeks red, his chest pumping for air, arms and legs flailing.

The applause grew louder and the cheering began.

Go, Jeffrey, keep running man.

The first four runners gathered at the finish line. People began running beside Jeffrey as on he came, running to give him hope, to let him know they cared, cheering him on, clapping as they ran beside the stumbling youth.

One woman ran beside Jeffrey, tears streaming down her cheeks as she watched him work out.

At the finish line, perhaps two dozen people had gathered to welcome the last-place runner.

Jeffrey crossed that finish line, his wavering arms thrust into the air, met there by a mob of well-wishers, all hugging and patting him on the back, some openly crying, others straining to see through a mist of tears.

We were so damn proud of Jeffrey.

On the back of his T-shirt was printed the words, "Let me win, but if I cannot win, let me be brave in the attempt."

There is no better motto for the 1979 Wake County Special Olympics.

There were no losers. Some threw balls farther then others. Some jumped with ease while others struggled to stand upright. Some ran like deer, others could hardly walk in a straight line.

The retarded young men and women who completed at Sanderson High School gave it all they had for a strip of brightly-colored ribbon they could pin proudly to their chests.

The Special Olympics is David, a young boy from Garner. He was quiet, a mystery locked behind those far-away eyes, he never spoke, but he sat close beside me, watching the events. Shyly an arm snaked around my waist and he hugged me so gently my heart almost broke. He had his own way of communicating.

The Special Olympics is a mother from Knightdale. "I usually cry a couple of times here, but it's wonderful," she said. She would cry again that day.

The Special Olympics is Leon, a first-place winner in the softball throw, waving his ribbon for everyone to see, high above his head like a trophy. He was a winner, perhaps for the first time in his life (but not the last) and he wanted everyone to know it.

The Special Olympics is Chris, running the 50-yard dash one way and then turning and running back to the starting line to even bigger cheers. He wasn't supposed to, but that didn't matter. He had tasted glory and wanted more.

The Special Olympics is Jack, off to a bad start in the 50, coming from behind, staggered and wavering, but running hard to win the race and then he kept on running, off the track, around a truck and running on until he was caught in the loving arms of a volunteer.

The Special Olympics is Lucy, turned around the wrong way at the starting line, confused when the gun went off, finally getting turned around and running in the right direction, stopping just before she crossed the finish line because she didn't want to break the string and finally ducking under it and when told she'd won, shouting, "I really took off, didn't I?"

The Special Olympics is a place of hugs and tears and love and trying ... and winning.

Wilmington.

It was an October afternoon, a day of sharply focused white clouds against a Carolina Blue sky.

It was easy to walk that day, easy to think nothing could be wrong on such a delicious day, easy to stroll along the waterfront and think of nothing in particular.

I came on it suddenly. There it was, a dark and seemingly sinister place on a beautiful day. The bar smell drifted out onto the sunny sidewalk. Looking inside, I could see people, hunched over cans and bottles, quietly talking.

It looked like a dive, a bar from an old movie about waterfronts and thugs and fallen angels. I knew Bogart must be in the back booth.

He wasn't. An old man sat at the front of the bar. He was talking to a barmaid who didn't hear him. He spoke of women and fights and old friends and she stared out the open door. Right in the middle of a sentence she would get up, walk to the back and to the front again, the slow story he told never faltering. He never knew she had left.

It was dark in the bar. The walls were mostly black, the light coming from illuminated beer signs. The only bright light came from the open door, bright light slashing into the darkness. It bathed the drinker's back and gave the barmaid a window to the sunshine.

Then came another man, this one short and drunk-feisty. A faded red washcloth was in his right hand and he mopped his face time after time, although it wasn't hot enough to sweat. He'd mop with his right and sip from the can with his left, the can touching his lips moments after the cloth left. Sip, swipe, sip, swipe. He never missed a beat.

"My son came home the other day and said, 'Daddy,

I've caught you drunk again,' '' he told us, although we hadn't asked. "He said to me, 'Daddy, I've done my dead level best to see you sober just one more time before you die and here you are drunk again.'

"Well, I looked up at him and said, 'Good buddy, don't you worry about it. Don't you worry about nothing.'

"He caught me by surprise. Sure, I was drunk. I was so drunk I couldn't do nothing but stand there, but he didn't have to talk to me like that, did he? What I do ain't none of his business. I can get drunk if I want to, ain't that right?''

No one answered. The first man launched into a long story about how he had dated the feisty man's first, or maybe it was his second, wife before he had.

"That was sure a pretty little girl," the first man recalled in his beer memory. "But that was a long time ago. You ever see her?''

"Naw, I ain't seen her and don't want to," the little man said. "Woman walks out on me and I'm done with her. She was all the time after me about my drinking. She told her Ma she'd married an alcoholic and then left me, but you're right, she was a pretty little thing, all right."

It was silent in the bar. The old men remembered the pretty little girl they had known, the barmaid looked out at the sunshine and the juke box was silent.

This was a place for drinking, not entertainment. Beer had brought them there the first time and beer would keep them there now.

They hadn't seen the sunshine in a long, long time.

Grantsville.

Mike Bradshaw trudged through the six inches of snow and mud that clung to him in sticky, bone-chilling layers.

"I told my fiance that I had to come," the 20-year-old resident of the Grays Chapel community said. "I keep thinking what it would be like if that was my little girl in there."

Bradshaw had just finished 24 hours standing in the mud that borders Lacy C. Kearns's 3-acre pond. He was only one of hundreds of weary men and women who had been searching for 10-year-old Tammy Kearns since she disappeared.

All through the search, the only evidence was a red and white tobaggan — Tammy's hat — the one she was wearing when she told her mother she was going to build a snowman in the 10 inches of snow that had blanketed this Randolph County community.

"That's all we've got, that tobaggan," Randolph County Sheriff Robert R. Masons said.

The hat, frozen in an inch-thick coat of ice on Kearns's pond was found the day before.

The search for Tammy Kearns began two days before when the girl did not return from her snowman-building expedition in the picture postcard setting of rolling hills and black angus cattle that surrounds the Kearns home.

Sheriff Mason nodded toward the pond where three ducks cruised gently in the muddy water.

"She used to feed those ducks in bad weather," the sheriff said. We think maybe she came down to feed them and fell in."

Hundreds of volunteers, most of them farmers and neighbors, criss-crossed the snowy woods as far as five miles from the Kearns house. They found nothing.

Teen-age members of the Civil Air Patrol, National Guardsmen, volunteer firefighters and rescue workers from two counties joined the search the second day.

Every home within five miles was checked as were all the homes of Tammy's fifth-grade classmates. Nothing.

"There's nothing left to do now but search the pond," Sheriff Mason said, while pumps drained the 20-foot-deep pond.

All eyes were on the still surface of the pond that afternoon as heavy fog and light rain joined the mud and grim searchers in a frigid, nightmarish scene.

Two boats with three men each probed the depths, using drag lines, each with five four-prong hooks. Back and forth they went, stopping when something was hooked. It was always a log.

As each hook caught, quiet conversation on the muddy banks stopped, all eyes on the searchers, only to turn away when the hooks came up empty.

"This is getting too close," Lacy Kearns told a searcher about mid-day as the level of the pond dropped. "I've got to go to the house."

Kearns had not slept for three days, Sheriff Mason said. "That poor man has walked the roads looking for Tammy ever since."

The hundreds of civilian volunteers, most of whom did not know Kearns or Tammy and some of whom came from 20 miles away, kept up the search around the muddy pond.

A fireman, muddy and wet, kneeled by a pile of burning tires used for heat, paying no attention to the the acrid black smoke that surrounded him.

A two-day stubble of beard framed the cigarette he pulled on deeply.

"Where is she?" he muttered to the fire. "Where in God's name is she?"

The answer came that night. Tammy Kearns's body was retrieved from the bottom of the pond.

Freewheeling

I hadn't thought of her in 20 years, but when I did, it was as if I had never forgotten.

Her face shone as clearly in my mind as it did that dawn, that gray morning down by the station.

I knew when I saw her that day that I'd never forget her. I might not have thought of her in 20 years, but I didn't forget.

I was at the train station early on that damp, chilly morning in 1956. My newspaper route took me by the station and I had met the same train before, I peddling my 265 News and Observers and the train heading south to Miami.

There was something exciting about those mornings when I met the train. I loved to stand on the platform and listen to the steam from the hissing train. On cold mornings the steam was heavier, creating a fog-shrouded world of people going somewhere.

The baggage handlers moved easily through the passengers and well-wishers. Their steel-wheeled baggage carts with big-spoked wheels rumbled across the cracked concrete, made wet in places by the steam.

Elegant black men, some in starched white jackets and some wearing formal blue uniforms stood by the car doors, placing their little steps in exactly the right spot without even looking. They grabbed every elbow that came down those steps, supporting and directing with the same five words: "Wilson, watch your step, please."

What a strange and marvelous job, I thought, to be able to travel all the time, not just on trips to see aunts and cousins. The places they went, I wanted to go. I was 14 and homesick for a place I'd never been.

The morning I saw her, I was sitting on an empty baggage cart, watching this tiny city on wheels as it came through my country town.

The lights in the coach car were dim that morning. Blurred figures behind sweating glass moved quietly in some cars, others were full of sleeping shapes.

An overhead light on the station platform made the steam shine brightly, puffy white clouds of wet heat. I moved off the cart and closer to the train, into the fog. It smelled like somewhere else.

She was facing north, her back to the engine. Her left arm was on a rest and her cheek rested on her closed fist.

Her eyes never moved. She was awake but she wasn't seeing. Five minutes later and she'd never remember stopping.

She was the most beautiful, perfect, incredible creature I have ever seen. To describe her would be impossible. If I said she had short, curly hair, would that help? I couldn't see the color of her eyes, I couldn't see below her neck. I never heard her voice or touched her skin. She had two eyes, a nose and a mouth.

She also had two hearts, hers and mine.

I stood there, captivated, seeing her enough in three minutes to last 20 years. I didn't wave or try to attract her attention. I only stared, a country boy seeing beauty for the first time.

The conductor standing beside me didn't even look at his watch, he just waved a lantern and the train moved.

The steam stayed still as the train lurched, disturbing the girl in the window. Her head moved forward a couple of inches and she moved her arm. She sat up straight quickly, her eyes darting to the window. And she looked at me.

I didn't move. I couldn't. I just looked.

Then she smiled and the train slowly left, taking the

steam, the porters, the conductor and the girl with it.

The only thing left were the wet places on the pavement and a memory.

She must have been a princess and whoever she is, and wherever she is, I sure do hope she's happy.

Big Wheels and Iron Men

A cold mist was chilling Raleigh that early morning, smearing windshields and making the cup of coffee in my hand give up a heavy head of steam.

Number 82 slid into the Seaboard Coast Line station, hissing and shaking the ground.

"You ready to go?" Carl Wicker asked. We walked down the long train, stopping at the ladder that would take us up to the cab of the engine. I grabbed the wet rails and pulled myself up. In a few moments engineer Jimmy Stephenson gave a yank on the whistle handle. A surge of power came through my shoes as he brought the two diesel engines to life. Slowly, almost at a walking speed, the train moved out.

It was right on time, as always. That's the way Stephenson does things.

The world looks different from the cab of a train. From the coach seats you see it flashing past. From the cab, perched high in the air, you see it coming straight at you, rushing down a thin ribbon of twin steel rails.

Even the towns look different. Motorists see clean streets and neatly manicured lawns. Railroad men see dirty back alleys and littered back yards. They see us as we are, not as we'd like others to see us.

Hitting speeds of up to 79 mph, the maximum allowable speed although 100 mph would be easy, we shot northward, slowing only for towns and repair work on the rails.

We rattled along, swaying gently from side to side over rough track, fairly gliding on. The speed seemed slow from so high in the air. Seventy on a train feels like 50 in a car.

Coming up to the Roanoke River, Stephenson put on the brakes. The orders said no more than 20 mph while repair work on the bridge continued, and railroad men always follow orders. Their lives depend on it.

Bridges are downright scary. No space is wasted. The wheels cling to the tracks, but the side of the cars hang over open space. From a half-mile away I wonder if that little bridge could hold up this monster. It can, but it seems to take forever.

Once we hit Virginia, Stephenson let her rip. We roared along on smooth rails slashing through a rainy, foggy morning.

Wildlife has learned the cruel lesson of highways and cars that kill, but they seem to like the tracks.

I see a huge wild turkey, something I have never seen before, waiting by the tracks in front of us. It waits until the last moment before rising up in front of us and heading for the deep woods.

Further along, a small herd of wild deer playfully races beside us before darting away to the leafy shadows.

The cab of a train is not a pretty place. It is cold metal and oily smells. The engineer sits on the right side, facing a panel of gauges, brakes, throttle and whistle controls. There are two seats on the left side, a water cooler in the middle and a toilet in a forward compartment. It is a place of work, with all the glamor of a boiler room.

"Working for the railroad can be a lot like living near a stinking paper mill," L. E. "Stormy" Weathers, an engineer, said. "You can get used to it, but you might not ever really love it.

"You've got to decide things like if a dentist appointment is worth two or three days' pay, because if they call you and you can't go because of a dentist appointment or something, then you don't get paid and you miss that trip. You only get paid if you're on a train. Being home for an anniversary could cost you a week's pay if the timing is wrong.

"It's romantic to some people, and I've been doing it for 37 years, but I could live without it."

Joe "Sally" Rand, an old-school brakeman who still wears denim, said, "It's not conducive to a good family life. A good railroad wife is the greatest woman in the world. She's got to be able to do without you a lot of the time, but bless my wife, everytime I've come home or left, she's been there to fix me something to eat."

Like men on any job, they have fears, the things that weigh on their minds on those long runs when they are tired and the tracks seems endless.

"Sometimes you come to a crossing and you'll see a big log truck pull up to the crossing and then pull right out in front of you," Jimmy Stephenson said. "You might not be going but 50 miles an hour, but it seems like 150. All you can do is grab the brakes and the whistle and see if it happens this time. There ain't nowhere to go."

For Rand, the fear is school buses.

"God, I hope I don't ever hit one of them," he said. "That could make me leave the railroad. The other thing is a gas truck. You can't help but think about it sometimes. You go down the track after a wreck and pick up a shoe with a foot in it and you think about it. But what can we do? We sure can't turn."

But in each of them, in a dark corner that only comes out in moments of solitude, lies a young boy in love with trains.

"I would like to take me one more run on a steam engine," Rand said. "You look back and see that smoke hanging over the train when you go around a curve, and that's something to see."

The ride home is much the same, only much slower and with more rain.

I stand in the rain, looking up at the giant that has brought me home, bone tired with a taste of too many cigarettes and too many yelled words rasping my throat.

And I love trains more than ever.

Rust Never Sleeps

Remember that story in the paper a few years ago about the Japanese soldier in the Pacific who had laid low in the jungles for 30 years — because he never got the word that the war was over?

That should have been my first clue.

If I had figured it out then I could have saved myself a lot of money, temper tantrums, ulcer medicine and frayed nerves.

What I have figured out is there is yet another Japanese

soldier hiding out, a never-say-die son of the emperor who not only has not surrendered, but is even today engaging in guerrila warfare in our fair land.

But he is not a flesh and blood soldier.

He is a car.

The best I can figure out is that when World War II was almost over the Japanese generals dispatched a robot to infiltrate the United States. The robot's job was to hide out until the early 1970s. And then, when gas supplies became short and cars became small, the robot was to disguise itself as an import car.

The robot did his job. It became a car in 1973.

Would you like to guess who bought that car?

You got it. Me.

It began when my beloved 1960 Corvair with the wooden floorboard was ambushed by a pickup truck. I went to Fast Eddie's to buy a new one.

All of them had been sold, he said, except for one way out on the back lot. If that was the last one, I should have reasoned then maybe there was a good reason no one else had bought it.

There was, as it turned out, but I bought it anyway.

It didn't take long.

The first thing it did was die in the middle of Interstate 95 at 11:30 on Sunday night. I found out, after I paid $15 to be towed in, that while every other of that breed had a 10-gallon gas tank, I had one with a six-gallon tank.

That meant I was out of gas when the needle said I still had almost a half tank.

Then one cold morning I started my car to let it warm up in the driveway. The minute my back was turned it rolled down the driveway and criminally assaulted my neighbor's Buick to the tune of $800.

Not bad for a car that cost only $2,500.

Exactly 10 days after I got it out of the car hospital, it sent out a magnetic ray and sucked a big Ford into my back seat.

This is all true. I have witnesses.

It went on. And on.

Once I was offered a great job. Halfway between my house and the prospective boss' office, the car decided it did not want to move, so it died, this time at 1 p.m. on a Saturday when every garage is closed.

That aborted trip cost me the job, over $500 in repair bills and two months without a car.

Then the water pump fell off. I got so mad I slammed the door and the window fell out. I plopped back down in the seat and the seat back broke.

Paint is now coming off in large pieces, leaving me with the only naked car in my neighborhood. The taunts of neighborhood children have been cruel.

Then I bent the key after the door lock jammed. Then I pulled the emergency brake completely out of the car, leaving a gaping hole in the floorboard.

It went blind one night and not a single light would work and I was three miles from home and it was 1 a.m.

The next time some yo-yo brags that his car has gone 150,000 miles on two quarts oil and a Band-Aid, I'm going to run over him.

If I can get my car started, that is.

I should have known it would happen.

A few months back I wrote a column about my accursed car, which I accused of being a Japanese robot sent to this county to bedevil the poor fool in whose driveway it lived.

The weird thing was, from that day on, my car has been a real champ, purring its way literally from Murphy to Manteo with nary a bump, groan or wheeze.

It was waiting for the right moment to pay me back.

The right moment came five minutes past noon on a blustery Sunday in January in probably the most isolated place in North Carolina: four miles north of Rodanthe, on the Outer Banks.

The moment the car slowed I knew I was in a heap of trouble. There was a certain finality about the silence when the motor stopped. I could tell it would never run again, at least not that day.

So there I sat, as far from home as I could get, with a storm expected within hours (it eventually covered the spot where I sat with a lot of very cold ocean).

I was, quite frankly, feeling very sorry for myself, and for good reason, as it turned out.

John Blizzard, the public relations fellow for Dare County, came to my rescue after I cried into the telephone. Heck, I didn't mind crying if it would help. What else could I do? Sit there and drown?

Within a brief hour and a half, Blizzard had found two truckloads of mechanics who drove all the way down from Kill Devil Hills to rescue me. They poked, nodded, hummed a lot and said, "Try it now."

I did. More silence.

They were super mechanics and knew exactly what was wrong with my car. The only problem was, they don't sell parts for my car south of New Jersey; even there, you can get them only on alternate Tuesdays when the moon is full.

Few things are sadder than following a wrecker as it tows your car to a garage. I silently hoped they would drop it into Oregon Inlet. I even suggested it would make a dandy reef for the fish. But they made it back to Manteo and that's when I was faced with how in heck I was going to get home again.

Then someone mentioned the bus.

Riding a bus is about as much fun as watching a Loretta Young film festival, especially when you ride for three hours in a direction you don't want to go so you can get on a bus for four hours in the direction you do want to go.

The bus station in Norfolk is not my favorite spot on the planet. It's nice enough, I guess, but there isn't much to do once you've counted the luggage lockers.

The bus came, finally, and as we crawled aboard — dirty, hungry, ill-tempered, sleepy and bored — it was raining harder than I remember ever seeing it rain. That allowed my paranoia to run wild, expecting to be hit broadside by a screaming, out-of-control, 18-wheel, fire-breathing truck driven by a deranged dope fiend.

We weren't, and we arrived in Raleigh 16 hours after the car died, even more bored, ill-tempered, dirty, hungry and sleepy than before.

Then I made the trip all over again, in reverse, to go back and pick up the car when the work was finished.

That trip went fine, except for one thing.

When I got to Manteo, got my car out of hock, thanked everyone profusely and prepared to return to high ground, I realized my luggage had been lost.

But the car runs fine. For now.

Four-Wheel Fantasies

She looked sad sitting there in the slush, battered, rusty, sagging ever so slightly on her left front wheel, finally come to the end of the road.

This was it — she had been traded in on a new model, a spiffy silver thing that looks like it's going 50 mph when it's sitting still.

I paused as I walked away from my little brown car. For a brief moment I thought back over the nearly 70,000 miles we had gone together, most of them in the past two years. For a tender moment I felt sorry for the little car. It had done its job well, with distinction and honor. It deserved to hold its dented head high up there in Good Car Heaven, and here it was, abandoned like so much worn-out machinery and rubber, far from home, alone in the cold, dark night.

It had served me well, gone where I'd asked it to go (mostly), done it inexpensively (even when gasping for breath, it would get 35 miles per gallon) and, in its younger days, it had enough zip to turn the occasional head as this smart-aleck, little upstart of an Oriental import won the occasional stoplight challenge (for the first 50 feet at least).

All of this flashed through my mind as I stood there in the snow. I thought kind things about my little car for all of two seconds. Goodbye, clunker, and long may you rust.

There is nothing that will pick up the February blues quicker than a new car.

There is no sense to it. When I bought my brown car five years go, I paid a whopping $2,500 for it, brand new off the boat, no discount, no wheeling and dealing, just sticker price. Now I have just spent almost three times that. I am so far in debt that my bank could open a new branch on what I'll be paying.

But I am so excited.

I started looking at new cars a couple of weeks back. Logic told me to be sensible, look for durability, gas mileage, safety, resale value, remember your position, be middle-class, be dull.

That's what my mind said. My heart said phooey.

What I wanted, I knew, was exactly what Burt Reynolds drove in that ode to Southern macho of a movie called "Smokey and the Bandit." I even wanted the hat and the Sally Field option.

I wanted a car that would let me drive faster than anybody. Period. You never know when that kind of speed will come in handy, like going out for a loaf of bread during the commercial.

So there I was, torn between a Dullmobile that was so sensible you wanted to be ill or a Studmobile that would quicken hearts in any hamlet into which I ventured, prowling and growling down the road. Wanna go varoom with me, Betty Jean?

But — and this is a little-known fact — any man with teen-age daughters must bring a note signed by his wife before the salesman will even let him drive one of those Machomobiles.

But what my lust for power did do was condition my wife that I wanted spiff this time. It is sort of like negotiating. I had Sensible Wife so scared I was going to come roaring up in the driveway with a car that spit flames that she was actually relieved when I brought home My Baby.

That's what I've named her, and I am shameless in my fondness for her. Man should not love machines; he should use them. Right. I love my new car. It is silver (not gray smarty-pants, but gleaming, sexy, sparkling silver, or so it says here in my brochure). It has gadgets galore, and I truly love gadgetry.

I've not only got a windshield wiper on the rear window, I've got a gizmo that lets you know when a door is ajar. And it tells you which one by flashing a picture of the car on a tiny little screen with the offending open portal in bright red on a field of green.

I demonstrated the gadget to Sensible Wife.

"Look," I bubbled excitedly as she opened the door on her side. "Look at that," pointing to the computer display on my dash. There was her door, bright red like the guy said it would be.

"It would seem that you would know if your door was open, especially if you were half out of the car with your feet on the snow, wouldn't you?" she said sweetly. A little too sweetly I thought.

It was that kind of sensible thinking that killed the Corvair, the convertible and cars with tailfins.

People like that have the foolish notion that cars are just for transportation.

What a boring idea.

Landfall

It can be a savage land, when the storms of late summer scream out of the Caribbean and, the mighty Atlantic Ocean rises and slaps these barrier islands with a watery fist.

It is a land of incomparable beauty, towering sand dunes graced by stubborn sea oats, the way hair clings to a balding man.

It is a place where memory is more real than fact, the mosquitos are dreadful, the sun scorching, the water has a funny smell. You've seen few traffic jams to rival the ferry dock in Hatteras on holidays.

But it is a magic land, tall tales, flinty men and women, a curious Elizabethan brogue, men who challenge the sea to save the unlucky and unwise.

Blackbeard, The Graveyard of the Atlantic, Torpedo Junction, The Lost Colony, Diamond Shoals, heroes and fools, all of these and more.

They are the legendary Outer Banks.

It was barely 8:30 p.m.

Around the small building in Rodanthe, people were jammed oyster shell to beer can, slurping up half-raw oysters and bring-your-own spirits with enough gusto to make a television beer commercial jealous.

Inside the old house turned community center, a laidback country band everyone said was from "up north in Norfolk" brought the crowd alive when they hit the first notes of Texas-style homegrown boogie.

"Half these people don't really know what's going on and the other half don't care," an avid newcomer to the Outer Banks said above the din. "This is the biggest party of the year and it won't be long before the fights start."

They had already begun.

Not that they could have hurt each other seriously. One Banker took a swing at another, connected with the aimed-for chin, and then both men fell, one possibly from the glancing blow, the other from the brew.

As far as anybody could tell, the reason for the fight was that one man was young and the other man wasn't. It doesn't make much sense but that's what they said, and with fists flying, nobody was about to ask for details.

The official purpose for all of this was the annual celebration of Old Christmas in this tiny island village, perched delicately between the Atlantic and the Pamlico Sound. Every year for longer than anyone can remember their folks telling them about, the people here have gathered on Jan. 5 to celebrate Christmas on the day it used to be before somebody monkeyed with the calendar a couple of centuries back.

The traditions go back as far as the celebration and no one knows where they came from either. But the reason they do it is simple: that's the way they've always done it and why change?

"Wasn't nobody out here but the Bankers then, and it was a good time. Everybody looked forward to it all year," John Herbert, at 80 the oldest man in Rodanthe, said.

They still do.

Out in the yard, with a heavy fog shutting out the rest of the world, these people of the island scuffled, ate oysters, drank beer, danced to country music, and remembered.

That's the way they'd always done it, and that was reason enough.

The year was 1585.

Sir Richard Grenville of Cornwall was on his way to Virginia, which is what the English called all the new lands across the sea.

His ship, the Tyger, put into what is now Puerto Rico to pick up supplies for the last run to Roanoke.

According to the official narrative of the trip, he picked up "horses, mares, kine (cattle), sheep and swine."

Fully loaded, the Tyger made its way carefully up the coast of what is now North Carolina's Outer Banks and then turned inland, heading for Pamlico Sound.

Coming through Ocracoke Inlet the Tyger ran aground, as so many of the ships that followed would do. Grenville had to put ashore for repairs.

The animals, which were carried on deck, were put over the side for the swim to the island since there were no docks.

And a legend was born.

The ponies of Ocracoke had found a home. The first permanent residents had to swim ashore, a tradition that continues.

The Bankers have always been people of the sea. They fish, they serve on ship's crews, the men of the Outer Banks are eagerly sought as members of the U. S. Coast Guard.

The stories they tell are tales of the sea.

His glasses are thicker now, and the graying hair sweeps back smoothly from a high forehead.

"We'd go up and down the coast in all kinds of weather," C.Q. Willis said. "It's awfully fatiguing to work 24 hours a day, day after day, on a fishing trawler, but that's what we did, and that's what they do now.

"We'd go for weeks at a time and never pull off our foul weather gear.

"You'd work so long that when you looked up at the sky, it would look yellow. You're in bad shape then.

"On a trawler you've got to work when you find the fish, no matter when it is. We'd be out there when it was 25 degrees and the wind blowing 20 knots. You'd take one step on deck and freeze. We used to huddle around the muffler on the deck engine just to keep from dying.

"If you'd get a chance, you'd go below and die for 15 minutes in a bunk and then someone would bang on the wall and you'd stagger back out like a dead man and keep doing it again.

"It wasn't all bad times. Sometimes when bad weather came up we'd go to Ocracoke. That harbor would be full of trawlers, side by side, all over it.

"The people would say, 'Hey, the fleet's in' and we'd have us some parties. Sometimes they'd show movies at the old Washab Coffee Shop (now the gracious Island Inn). They might not be very new movies, but we'd go.

"The Coast Guard boys would sell whiskey. They'd sell it for $10 a fifth. I don't know how many times I've paid that and I was glad to do it."

When the weather turns bitter cold and the off-shore winds whip the ocean into an icy fury, there is a saying that "It's gonna get colder than the night the Crissie Wright went ashore."

She was 800 tons, a three-masted schooner out of Baltimore, bound for Savannah, her spacious holds loaded with guano.

Capt. Thomas P. Clark and his crew had rounded Cape Fear, Cape Lookout ahead. There were six men in the Crissie Wright's crew.

She was five miles offshore, coming around Cape Lookout when the northeastern sky turned deadly black. Heavy clouds began to build. The trouble had begun.

Capt. Clark turned the proud ship toward shore. He

knew the reputation of Diamond Shoals, lying dead ahead, and he chose not to test its wrath this stormy day.

The ship raced the weather for safety, but as Clark neared protected waters, the wind began to scream in the rigging. Sails ripped like tissue paper, control was lost. The Crissie Wright was dying.

She hit stern first, smashing into a reef, stuck tight, her proud bow facing the storm and taking seas over her, stem to stern. Slowly, the pounding sea did its work. The Crissie Wright was turned until she lay broadside to the storm's fury.

Now all that could be done was save the crew. Clark ordered his men up the mast and told them to lash themselves to the timbers and ride out the storm. To have stayed on deck would have meant being washed overboard to sudden death. In the rigging, maybe there was a chance.

The wind roared on, gale force now, battering the men and the ship into senseless cold. The temperature was falling fast. It was a full January gale, a killing storm. The temperature soon stood at eight degrees.

People on the beach watched the horror of the sea and cold. They built a huge bonfire, but there was little else to be done. There were no lifesaving stations, only the whalers of Diamond City, and they faced raging winds and waves 10 feet high. Any whaler who challenged the sea this night would die.

Throughout the long night, the men were whipped by the freezing wind, rain and ocean, holding on for their lives. All they could see was the bonfire burning. It was hell on the sea, numbing cold, smashing winds and 200 yards away ... warmth, safety and people.

They were still there at dawn, the dying crew of the Crissie Wright, seven tiny figures in the ship's rigging, silhouetted against the sky.

And then there were six.

Capt. Clark was the first to die. He froze to death on the mast and fell into the sea. His body was not recovered.

The cold drove two crewmen to madness, it is supposed, and they tried to climb down and go below decks. They were lost overboard.

The four remaining crew members wrapped themselves in a sail and hung on, waiting for the end, either safety or the release of death.

Whalers Seef Willis and John Lewis challenged the sea shortly after dawn and made it to the Crissie Wright.

There were no signs of life.

Finally they spotted the bulge in the sails and found the remaining four crew members.

Three of them had frozen to death, wrapped in one another's arms to capture what heat was left.

But one, the cook, was alive. He was taken ashore.

The three men who froze to death were buried together, in a common grave.

And the ship? Her bones are still there, just off shore. On a very low tide, it is said, you can see her, lying in the spot where the proud Crissie Wright came ashore on that cold, cold night.

But not all wrecks ended in disaster. The Midgetts of Chicamacomico often challenged the sea and won.

On a stormy, blustery afternoon, Aug. 16, 1918, the British tanker Mirlo, under the command of Capt. William R. Williams, was making headway around Cape Hatteras, heading north to Norfolk with a load of gasoline and 52 seamen.

On the beach, the men of the Chicamacomico Lifesaving Station, under the command of Capt. John Allen Midgett, were going about their routine duties. Surfman Leroy Midgett was on watch in the lookout tower and John Herbert was in the kitchen, preparing for the evening meal.

They were moments away from becoming legends.

The German submarine U-117 also was on duty that day, laying mines off the North Carolina coast. The sub spotted the Mirlo as she rounded the cape and at 3:30 p.m. fired a single torpedo.

The torpedo hit the Mirlo amidship, the gasoline exploding in a rolling ball of black smoke and orange flame. Capt. Williams, a veteran seaman, knew his ship was dying and he ordered the Mirlo beached, hoping to save his crew. But two more explosions ripped through the tanker and Williams ordered his men to abandon ship in the heavy seas.

Surfman Leroy Midgett had seen the first explosion and within minutes the six men of surfboat crew 1046 were fighting their way through the heavy surf, trying to reach the men of the Mirlo.

Three times those Bankers charged into the rolling surf and three times the sea beat them back. Finally, in one last desperate attempt, the surfmen cleared the breakers and headed for the burning ship.

Meanwhile, the crew of the Mirlo had abandoned ship in four lifeboats. One of the boats capsized, throwing the men into the ocean. The three lifeboats still afloat tried to reach the men clinging to the overturned boat, but suddenly, without warning, Hell came to the Atlantic.

Another explosion ripped through what was left of the Mirlo, igniting the barrels of gasoline still on her decks and setting fire to the sea itself, now covered by oil and gasoline. The blaze caught the men clutching the overturned lifeboat in the ring of fire. There was no escape, nothing to do but wait until they either burned to death or drowned.

The men in the other three boats did all they could, but there was no reaching their shipmates, so Capt. Williams ordered the lifeboats to safety, trying not to hear the screams of the men who would die.

But into this inferno of burning oil, billowing smoke and screaming seamen came the surfmen of Chicamacomico, their surfboat chugging through the heavy seas. Capt. Johnny, as he was called, immediately saw what was happening.

As the surfmen approached the wall of flames, barrels of gasoline continued to explode, sending sheets of burning oil 100 feet into the air and pouring more flames onto the burning sea.

But luck, or God, was with them all that day and Capt. Johnny spotted an opening in the burning water and slowly brought the wooden surfboat through the flames.

Surrounded by fire, the surfmen pulled six hysterical men from what had seemed certain death and within six hours had saved 42 of the 52 men of the Mirlo.

The Outer Banks can be eerie at times. Stand near the point at Ocracoke and sometimes, when the fog rolls in, they say you can see the ghost of Blackbeard, come to claim the treasure some say he buried near here.

And stand at Hatteras, looking out at the foam and chop of Diamond Shoals and wonder what happened to the Carroll A. Deering and the Sea Quest. The stories are true, the mystery unsolved.

She will go down in history as the Ghost Ship of Diamond Shoals, the greatest mystery of the graveyard of the Atlantic.

It was early morning, a stormy, blustery day, that 31st day of January in 1921. The sea was rough; the waves battering the beaches.

Surfman C. P. Brady was the lookout at the Cape Hatteras Coast Guard Station, and he was nearing the end of his all-night shift, thinking of breakfast and a warm bed.

He looked one last time at Diamond Shoals, those churning breakers offshore. And he saw something that startled him.

There, only a half-mile offshore, was a beautiful ship, a five-masted schooner with all sails set, the last of her kind, built as the era of tall ships was ending. She was aground on the shoals, a lovely thing come to die.

Brady sounded the alarm. The Coast Guardsmen rolled from their bunks, taking to that stormy sea in open surf-boats as they had done so many times before.

The men could not reach the ship because the sea was too rough. They could not even get close enough to read her name.

They searched the beaches for survivors ... or bodies.

They found nothing.

Finally, a surfboat got close enough to read the name; she was the Carroll A. Deering, less than two years old, a sturdy ship, built in Bath, Maine. Shipping records would show she was on her way to Norfolk from Barbados with no cargo aboard.

The Coast Guardsmen looked for the crew. From all they could tell, the Deering had been abandoned. There was no one on deck; no one answered the hailing.

It was two or three days before the seas calmed enough for men to board the Deering, and when they did, they found a dead ship.

There was no one on board.

Down in the galley, the rescuers found that the table was set with dishes. There was food in the serving bowls.

On the stove were pots and pans, all with food in them.

A search of the crew's quarters was fruitless. Everything was shipshape, stored away as it should have been. Neat, the way seamen live.

Up on deck, there was more of the same. Lines were neatly coiled; pins were in place; the sails were rigged tauntly, as they should have been.

Several things were missing, however. Both anchor lines had been cut. All lifeboats were gone. The sextant was nowhere to be found.

Finally, members of the boarding party made their way below deck. There, they found something that has haunted seamen ever since. The steering cables that connect the wheel to the rudder had been cut, sliced neatly as if by an ax.

And to this day, not one piece of evidence, not one lifeboat, not one body, nothing that could be identified as having come from the Carroll A. Deering has been found.

Even today, when the sky and sea are right, her bones rise from the churning water, and people still wonder what happened.

John and Anna Fielding must have been scared to death that stormy night in the fall of 1976.

Heading north up the coast off North Carolina's Outer Banks, through the eerie seas that have taken so many ships and lives, they heard a crash.

Fielding rushed forward on the Sea Quest, a 41-foot sailing yacht. He looked through the spray kicked up by the high winds and rough seas and saw that the cable from the boat to the end of the thin bowspit out front had snapped.

Then the main cable supporting the mast gave way and the Sea Quest was in trouble, serious trouble. It looked as if the Graveyard of the Atlantic would claim more lives.

On board with the Fieldings was their 7-year-old daughter, Mary Jo. Anna, from Denmark, was pregnant.

John Fielding, an engineer in his mid-40s from San Francisco, went below on the Sea Quest, afraid of what he might find. It was possible, even likely, that he was taking on water through a crushed hull. But that night, luck was with the Fieldings. There was no sign of water coming in.

But the mast teetered precariously in the high winds, control was difficult and John Fielding called for help.

The Coast Guard station at Ocracoke heard their "Mayday" call and immediately launched a rescue boat and crew.

Now all the Fieldings had to do was keep the Sea Quest afloat and direct the Coast Guard to them.

Out of the storm appeared lights.

Fielding radioed the source of the lights, which turned out to be a freighter plowing its way along the coastline.

The freighter came alongside the Sea Quest to look for hull damage and to offer assistance as men of the sea will do for each other.

Fielding spoke to the captain of the freighter and through the storm could read the name of the ship painted on the bow and stern.

The Coast Guard heard Fielding talking to the crew of the freighter and interrupted to ask Fielding to determine the freighter's exact location to make rescue easier.

Fielding did as he was asked and relayed the information to the Coast Guard.

Then the freighter, assured that the Coast Guard was lined up for the rescue, went on its way. Moments later the Coast Guard arrived and escorted the Fieldings to safe harbor in Ocracoke, where the family would remain for nine months, waiting for the weather to clear, the boat to be repaired and the baby to be born.

But there was one question that will plague John and Anna Fielding as long as they live.

When they arrived on shore they were asked for the name of the freighter that had helped. Apparently the Coast Guard had been unable to hear what the freighter's crew was saying via radio, although they could hear Fielding's end of the conversation.

Fielding gave the Coast Guard the name of the ship and of the captain to whom he had spoken that night when death was on the winds.

He was told that the ship he claimed had helped, indeed under the command of the captain he had named, had sunk, in that same area, years before.

World War II came closer to the Outer Banks than anywhere else in North Carolina. Long called the Graveyard of the Atlantic, the seas off the Banks took on a new name, Torpedo Junction.

Nell Wise Wechter was there:

"I was teaching school in Buxton during World War II.

"It was called Torpedo Junction from all the ships that were sunk by the German submarines.

"Sixty ships sunk in a month right in our front yard wasn't unusual in those terrible days.

"I stood on the beach and watched the ships burning. The whole ocean looked like it was on fire for miles and miles.

"One night we were eating supper when we heard boom, boom, boom. In 30 minutes it looked like day from all the ships burning. The Germans had hit a convoy of ships hauling high-octane gas. Six ships sank that night.

"Bodies used to wash ashore, and one day we found an inflatable boat from the Germans. People thought they had come to sabotage the direction-finding station here.

"One day in school we heard the explosions start and I made everyone get under the desks. One little boy started yelling: 'We being bummed, we being bummed!' But another one yelled: 'Them ain't bums, those are ashcans (depth charges used against subs) and I ain't gonna miss it.' He took off for the beach and in a minute every one of them ran out to see.

"I figured I wasn't going to miss this, so here went the

teacher, chasing her flock to watch the Americans get the Germans. And they were right off shore, water was blowing 40 feet in the air when the ashcans went off. We never saw the sub, but in a little while we did see the oil slick come up on the beach, so they got him.

"But we didn't get many survivors from the ships making it to the beach. They either got picked up or died. How could they swim through a sea of fire?"

Things don't change much on the Banks. The schooners are all gone now, it is the age of diesel and ship-to-shore radio. There is a movie theater in Hatteras and four-wheel drive trucks prowl the beaches.

But at her heart, in her people, things haven't changed that much at all.

His name is Dan Robinson, a 37-year-old chief petty officer, and for the last 20 years he has been quietly going about his job of saving lives and ships:

"It can get exciting sometimes.

"You can get excited and you can get scared. When you've got a man sinking in the ocean and you cross that bar with the waves breaking and the boat bucking under you, you sometimes wonder why in the name of God you ever joined the Coast Guard.

"You get a boat in trouble and you go out and bring him in. That is beneficial to him and it makes you feel pretty good. This is the best duty because this is why most of us joined."

When the radio crackles or the phone rings, they can get one of their three rescue boats under way in less than three minutes.

"It is the overdues that scare us the most," Robinson said. "Then we don't know what the situation is or even where to look. All we know is that someone left one place going to another and didn't get there.

"You never get used to pulling a body out of the water. You may do it a lot, but it bothers you every time.

"When a man calls us and he is in trouble in the surf line, the boys here know they have to put themselves in the same danger he is in to get him out. They have to face exactly the same risks he is facing to save him. That makes our boys cautious.

"I don't know where you draw the line between saving your crew and the man you are trying to rescue, but we've got a job to do and we'll do it, one way or the other.

"They say our job is to save lives. It doesn't say anything about coming back ourselves, but so far we have.

"These kids, and they are the Coast Guard, the traditions and the future, like to do this work. When nothing is going on they'd rather be on a rescue than shining brass. It is an adventure for them. They might complain sitting around here, but they don't complain when we go to work.

"They are better educated and trained and have better equipment than coast guardsmen have ever had. These boys here are damn good.

"But we get as scared as anyone else when it's rough out there and we're trying to get to a guy.

"Any man who doesn't get scared doesn't respect the sea and that man can get you killed.

"These men respect the sea."

The sun hangs low in a vanilla sky, a blazing ball aging from white to gold.

Slowly, so slowly, it begins to slide gracefully, going home for the night.

It splashes fire across the silver waters of the Pamlico, fire that touches the tips of ripples, making them sparkle in a shimmering highway from the shore to the horizon.

The mosquitoes are out early, easy prey for the darting martins that flash like fighter planes, diving, twisting, catching dinner on the wing in a whirling ballet in the fading light.

Laughing gulls, those most perfect and lovely of all sky creatures, wheel in the gathering dusk, hanging motionless in front of the now golden sun, then diving like hawks on the attack, pulling up at the last moment to hang still in the gentle sea breeze.

The sun is lower now; the path it paints on the sea narrows as the color deepens.

Now it is pure gold, so dark it looks tarnished with age. The wavelets still, the gold unbroken. Once it shimmered and sparkled, now it gleams smoothly.

On the horizon a boat heads home, a black shadow on the silver sea. It crosses the path of the sun, and for an all-too-brief moment it is silhouetted against the reddening sun.

The air is growing cooler as the sun nears the sea. The sun is all red now, fat and heavy, like an old man after dinner, gently heading for sleep.

It shines brightly for a moment longer, as if to say good-bye, and then plunges into the thick sky at the edge of the world.

The golden path it painted fades back to blue, and only a lavender pink cloud remains like a celestial footprint, marking the path of the sun.

Evening has come to Ocracoke.

The yachts lie heavy in the harbor; the sound of sailors at play rings out.

On board the Brigadoon a cocktail party bellows above the clink of glasses as good friends celebrate good boats and good harbors.

Visitors walk the docks, some holding hands, others holding thoughts, gazing at the millions of dollars floating by the quay.

The sailors smile back, secure in their wealth, knowing anyone ashore would change places with them in a moment.

The ferryboat crews gather as the sun fades, old hands and young voices making music.

They sing songs from the mountains they've never seen and songs of cheating women and barrooms and trains.

The rich and would-be rich leave their boats swaying on the evening tide, gathering quietly to hear these hard-working men make music as darkness falls and the blue sky turns black under a full moon.

A woman suddenly breaks into a joyous, foot-stomping clog, and the strings ring with new vigor. Goosebumps grow, fed by the night's exuberant beauty.

Then the music slows. A quartet sings "The Tennessee Waltz," then songs of faith, "He Touched Me" and "Because He Lives."

Their voices are pure and true, and the people are moved to silence, not breaking the spell woven of guitar strings and a night in Ocracoke.

It ends, all too soon.

Lights from across the harbor make icy scratches on the ebony waters; lines clank like wind chimes in the breeze amid mumbled good nights and final toasts by candlelight.

Ocracoke sleeps.

Closest to Home

We call her Maggie.

She is our dog. She came to live with us after my very sneaky wife tried to pull a fast one by bringing her home "just for the weekend."

Right.

Maggie was a stray. She came from nowhere to live outside my wife's office building. She would stand by the cafeteria window, wagging that funny tail of hers and doing her starving-dog imitation.

We used to have another dog, a creature named DiDi that was murdered by poison 10 years ago. She was a perfect dog and it took 10 years of looking before I found another that could take her place. I used to look at dogs and silently compare them to DiDi, but none ever measured up. To have loved a lesser dog wouldn't have been right. It's hard to be pleased when you've had the best.

Maggie came home with my wife that Friday afternoon, and I was met at the door with promises heaped upon promises that it was just for the weekend.

I walked into my daughter's bedroom, took a look at the bundle of fur and friendliness plopped in my daughter's lap, got my hand licked and thought long and hard about whether or not we should keep her. I must have thought about it for all of 30 seconds.

Maggie is what you would call an enthusiastic dog. She is ready for anything. Want to take a nap? Yessirreebob, Maggie will snuggle by your hip and sleep just as long as you'd like. Want to take a walk? Here we go, off on a leash-pulling, squirrel-chasing, neighborhood-exploring adventure. Want to play some ball? Watch me be silly and fall over when I try real hard but never quite get it right. She thinks kite flying is the most fun of all.

But the cat was not amused.

Frisky is the last of a family of four incredible cats who saw us through some hard times. She assumes that it is her mission on Earth to boss our family around. She has trained my wife so well that when she decides on a 2 a.m. stroll my wife can get up, let the cat out and go back to bed and never wake up.

Frisky, whose idea of exercise is yawning and stretching, took one look at Maggie and headed for the high country, up on the buffet. I did not know it was possible to travel all over my house without ever touching the floor, but Frisky found a way.

The dog would bounce and want to play. Frisky would scowl. The dog would want to smell noses, an honorable canine tradition, and the cat would snarl. I felt like Henry Kissnger trying to keep the Israelis and the Arabs apart. If you patted the dog's head, you had to scratch the cat's ears or she would eat a record album.

If you feed the dog, the cat had better get double portions or may the Lord have mercy on you. You don't know the meaning of the words "long night" until you have tried to pacify a cat with hurt feelings who wants to talk it over at 3:35 a.m.

But I caught her the other day, when no one was looking: Frisky walked up to Maggie and actually rubbed against her. Joy reigned in the house. The crisis was past. Caught in her moment of weakness, the cat looked embarrassed and suddenly was hit with a dirt attack and tried to act like all she was doing was washing herself.

Things have settled down a little more in recent days. The eight gerbils in one daughter's bedroom no longer have air-raid drills each time the dog comes in to check on them. The cat actually seems to sort of like the dog and the dog, of course, loves everyone and everything.

And I, a confirmed cat person, now am also a dog person. Just the other day, while running an errand, I took Maggie along, just for the company and we had a good time together, just the two of us.

I think DiDi would have understood.

Denise: Sixteen Candles

September 1, 1978.

For all the little girls about to become women, but mostly for their daddies ...

You looked at me that first day and I knew my life would never be the same again. It was in your eyes, blue eyes that would hardly focus.

Those baby eyes met mine for an instant and that special love between a daddy and his little girl began to grow.

I looked at you with uncertainty, that first day so long ago, maybe even with fear. I had never been a daddy before. No one had ever depended on me so completely. And I had never loved anyone that way before.

Husbands love wives, brothers love sisters, friends love each other, fathers love sons and mothers love daughters, but somehow, in ways that I don't understand, the love of a father for a daughter is special.

I watched with awe as you grew. Soon chubby hands grew strong, grasping my outstretched finger like a baseball bat as we played.

I could watch you then, without feeling self-conscious when you caught my eye, when you saw me staring, captivated by your magic.

I would throw you in the air, you giggling and your mother clucking worriedly behind us. You looked at me with such complete trust. You knew I wouldn't let you fall.

We played a lot in those days. There was more time, it seemed, more time to be a family. You rode miles on my knee, laughing as we rode to market on a silver horse and a father's dream.

And you kept on growing. Lace dresses replaced droopy diapers, and soon scruffy jeans replaced the dresses. You grew taller, more awkward. Your baby charm faded on a dusty playground.

Schoolbooks cluttered the house. Would you ever unlock the mystery of the multiplication tables? You sat hunched over, chewing on a random piece of hair, scribbling in that funny scrawl. Sometimes tears would come when it got too difficult. You tried so hard not to disappoint me. Sometimes I feared I was asking too much of one so young.

I knew I would lose you one day. I could tell when it started, but you probably never noticed. But one day you were in a hurry to go outside, there wasn't time to sit in your daddy's lap. I watched you run out to play, excitement in your eyes, a giggle in your voice. I was happy for you ... but not for me.

It wasn't all smiles. I have been strict, sometimes too much so. I have said no when my heart wanted to say yes. I have seen hurt in your eyes, and disappointment when neither of us lived up to the other's expectations. That's what happens when two people expect the other to be perfect.

There were times when I wanted to pick you up and shake you, like a puppy that had misbehaved. What was right was so easy to see, I wanted to shout, why can't you see it?

But I couldn't be you. I had to leave the pain of growing up to you. I could be there to wipe the tears or hold you close when the world slapped you down, but the pain was yours alone to bear.

I have stood outside your room and listened to you cry.

You didn't know I was there, the same way you didn't know I was there all those nights after you went to bed and I took a moment to stand in the shadows and watch you sleep. You didn't know I was there those nights when you cried out in your sleep, and I rushed to your room to make sure you were all right, your mother at my side.

Now we have to come to the next great plateau in our lives together. Today you are 16. Now you have friends of your own, a life outside our home. You even have a job, beginning to earn your own way.

I watch you now, and you still don't see me doing it. I watch as you become a woman, stealing a man's heart as you have so often stolen mine. I watch you as you learn to drive, cutting that last tie that binds.

For 16 years you have brought me exquisite joy, unbearable pain, numbing fear and, yes, flashes of anger.

But through it all, you have given me your trust and your faith. I have tried so hard to deserve them.

Now you are 16. My heart bursts with pride at the person you have become. You are mature, attractive, self-confident, eager to take on the world on the world's terms.

Growing up to be a young woman is not easy.

But then neither is growing up to be a daddy.

Melanie: Sweet Little Rock and Roller

Greensboro.

I watched her disappear into the surging crowd, eyes bright, so excited she could hardly stand it.

For a moment I thought about yelling: "Hey, wait a minute, don't go in by yourself. Let me help you."

But she was gone, and it was good that she was. If I had insisted on seeing her to her seat in the cavernous Greensboro Coliseum, both of us would have suffered for it, she from mortification, I from an overdose of parental concern.

It was a small thing, just one of those rites of passage we will go through together on her way to being a grown up. It was just as tough as I feared it would be.

After all, she's my little girl, my youngest, the one we always make believe will never grow up, to live forever as the baby of the family.

But babies grow up, too, don't they?

This was to be her big night, this blustery night in January with raw weather on the outside and her latest singing idol, Ted Nugent, on the inside.

It was her first major rock concert. Gone were the days when I held her hand as we found our seats for John Denver's gentle music.

No more little girl squeals and holding her up so she could see Donny Osmond.

Now it is a rangy guitar player, a "fox," I'm told, who sounds like a high-speed train wreck in four-four time.

This was her first Christmas without a stuffed animal under the tree. This year it was albums and a set of headphones, the latter for her pleasure and my sanity.

Discussion of the pending arrival of Mr. Nugent had gone on for a couple of weeks between my daughter and her best friend. They had discussed it all, from what to wear to what time we should leave Raleigh. Those two questions were enough to occupy hours of telephone time. How two 14-year-olds can spend three hours together, separate for five minutes to walk home, and then have to talk for another hour on the phone to bring each other up to date is beyond me.

Finally, the big day arrived. Normally, upon returning to my castle where everyone lets me think I am lord and master, I am greeted with waves of indifference. No one acknowledges that the king has returned.

This day was different. I was greeted with a shrill, "When are we leaving?"

I announced that our departure was imminent, knowing that if I delayed much longer the pair of them probably would melt.

We drove away, I alone in the front and they in the back like two grand dames on their way to high tea. They made faces and flirted outrageously as we passed cars and trucks. They bounced and screamed in two-part glee when something called "Freak Out" came on the radio four times on four different stations within an hour. In short, they were generally their normally lovable and obnoxious selves.

We stopped for food, and I watched amazed as two picky eaters downed a double handful of burgers, fries and drinks by the time I cleared the driveway. They looked like two vacuum cleaners stuck on high.

Nugent, known as the Motor City Madman, gave them their money's worth. It was high energy all the way, the music going from loud to pain. This music should be the theme song for World War III.

I waited anxiously in the lobby as the show ended. I had not known where my daughter and her friend were sitting. Had I known I would have spent the entire night watching them instead of the stage, a miserable way to spend three hours.

But here they came, grinning, bouncing, arms thrust in the air, screaming "great show" over and over again, yelling to other carloads of similarly inclined, blown-out fans, yelling that it was snowing, yelling just to tell the world they were in love with living.

It got quiet by the time we hit the edge of town. I glanced back over my shoulder and there they were, two sweet little rock 'n' rollers, slumped against each other, fast asleep, clutching their souvenir T-shirts the way they used to clutch teddy bears.

Growing up can be awfully tiring.

Mama: A Dove to Take Her Home

Mama died Saturday.

I want to tell you about her. We've shared many joys, many people, many places since this column began 30 months ago and I want to share my Mama and her life with you, for even in death, hers is still a story of life and love and joy.

I want to tell you something about her, maybe because I write a column for a living and I get to do that, maybe because by telling you I can lessen the pain I feel, the loneliness, the hurt. Maybe I'm being greedy; maybe it will be easier if you share it with me.

Her name was Lelia, born Williamson in 1892 in Wilson County. When she was 5, so the family story goes, a strapping, 22-year-old John Smith visited the Williamson home and bounced the laughing Lelia on his lap. Later they would wed, 17 years difference in their ages.

She loved John Smith. She loved him when they were young and on their farm having their seven children, she loved him when tuberculosis wracked his body, she loved him when he died, leaving her alone to raise the surviving six children.

And she loved him all through those long days and nights during the Depression when she was a young widow.

How she must have wept when she had to place her children in an orphanage, alone, unable to care for them. We would talk about it later, just she and I on those sunny afternoons after I was grown, when I'd skip work for an afternoon to visit, when my life got rocky and she was there to listen. Nothing she ever did hurt her as much as watching her and John Smith's children leave for the Free Will Baptist orphanage at Middlesex.

She knew the risks she was taking. Perhaps the children would never understand why their mother let them go like that, perhaps she would lose their love. But she knew there was no choice. Times were hard, and little children had to eat. It was survival.

It wrenched her soul and the scars never completely healed ... but she was so proud of what they became: There was Margaret, lovely and regal, who would later bear her own tragedies with strength; Pearl, tiny and gentle and wise; Joe, serious Joe, with his Mama's common sense; John, her youngest boy, the funny, jovial one; Elsie, the prettiest and the baby; and Daisy, beautiful and blonde, everyone loved Daisy.

I knew them all, except for Daisy. She was my mother and she died when I was 18 months old.

Mama didn't have to do it, everyone would have understood if she had begged off. She was 50 years old when Daisy died, leaving a scrawny baby son behind that someone had to raise. Her life had almost made itself pleasant. The children had survived the orphanage, times were better now, she had a new husband, she didn't need pain any more.

But she took me home, and for 19 years she struggled and scrimped and worked 10 hours a day in a laundry, a sweating inferno of a place, to raise a grandson. She worked at night and on weekends, making clothes for the wealthy. She sewed in department stores. She always had a garden. I can still see her bent over a hoe, urging that fertile earth to bring us food. We needed it.

Now she was Mrs. I.T. Lamm, married to a man whose strength matched hers. A hard, flinty man who, well into his 70s, decided to build a house on his own. Not only did he build the house alone, he made the cement blocks that went into the house and the wooden machine that made the blocks. And when he finished that house, he built another next door.

We didn't have a car. We didn't have a TV set. We

didn't have new clothes. I tagged along on the mule wagon when I.T. rode the streets of Wilson, peddling his bushels of fresh collards and turnip greens to black neighborhood grocery stores.

I guess those were hard times, but I didn't know it. Mama loved me so much it blotted out the notion that other families had more than we had.

Every now and then someone would get the idea that I should go live with my father and his new wife and I did, several times. Times were better when I did. I had nice clothes, a traditional family, there was nothing I could have wanted they wouldn't have given me. And Mama didn't have to worry.

But every time, I came back to Mama. I was greedy, I wanted her love, I didn't care how much sacrifice it meant to her. And she never turned me away. She was there with a bear hug and a kiss when I got off the train, worried on the inside, smiling welcome on the outside.

Soon there were just she and I again. I.T., years her senior, died and left us alone, just the two of us.

I left home at 19 and I don't think she was very happy about it. I had quit college and I was married. She didn't approve of either. Later she came to love my family as she had loved me, wholly, without reservation, she spoke of all of us with pride.

At age 69 she finally retired and her years were blessed. she traveled, visited family. She smiled more, now that there was time to relax.

She was into her 80s when she called us all and told us she had made a decision on her own. She would be moving into a rest home and she hoped we would respect her decision.

To the best of her memory — and it sparkled like her smile and witty nature — not one day passed in that rest home when she didn't have a visitor, perhaps a former neighbor, an old friend, a distant relative.

They came to see her to brighten her day, or so they told themselves, but all left knowing in their hearts she had done more for them than they had for her.

She simply made you feel good, whether she was playing piano for Sunday services at the rest home or just offering you an apple or a piece of candy from her endless bedside larder. She loved the children the most, a peck on the cheek from a grinning granny was just the ticket they needed.

Without exactly knowing why, everyone who knew her held her in awe. However they knew her, as Sister Lelia from the Contentnea Primitive Baptist Church; as Aunt Lelia, the matron of one of Wilson County's oldest families; as Miz Lamm, friend and neighbor or as Mama, the love she gave us all will never be forgotten.

It is easy to cry when I think of her, I have cried and will again, but that isn't true to her and what she was.

Hers was a life of joy, and we should all be thankful that in this life we were lucky enough to have known her.

She once told me a story I remember well. She was very sick, 86 years old and had had three heart attacks in as many days.

We thought we would lose her. In the darkest hours, when she had pulled deep down into herself, she remembered looking by her pillow and there, sitting by her head, was a little white dove.

"That little dove spoke to me and I felt complete peace," she said later, after her valiant heart had eased and she was getting better. "The dove told me not to worry, it wasn't my time yet. After that dove spoke to me, I started getting better."

None of us ever saw that dove, of course, and we were with her every moment, but she saw it. She had no doubts. And neither do I.

There was no one with her when she died Saturday. Her last visitor had just left her, and she was smiling as only she could smile.

But she didn't die alone. The little white dove that brought her such peace had come to take her home.

And I'll bet she was smiling.